surrender

surrender

SONYA HARTNETT

CANDLEWICK PRESS
CAMBRIDGE, MASSACHUSETTS

Copyright © 2005 by Sonya Hartnett

First U.S. paperback edition 2007

The Library of Congress has cataloged the hardcover edition as follows:
Hartnett, Sonya.
Surrender / Sonya Hartnett. — 1st U.S. ed.
p.   cm.
Summary: As he is dying, a twenty-year-old man known as Gabriel recounts his troubled childhood and his strange relationship with a dangerous counterpart named Finnigan.
ISBN 978-0-7636-2768-3 (hardcover)
[1. Family problems—Fiction. 2. Brothers—Fiction. 3. Dogs—Fiction.
4. City and town life—Fiction.]   I. Title.
PZ7.H267387Sur 2006
[Fic]—dc22   2005054259

ISBN 978-0-7636-3423-0 (paperback)

2 4 6 8 10 9 7 5 3 1

Printed in the United States of America

This book was typeset in Fairfield LH.

Candlewick Press
2067 Massachusetts Avenue
Cambridge, Massachusetts 02140

visit us at www.candlewick.com

For Dmetri Kakmi

GABRIEL

I am dying: it's a beautiful word. Like the long slow sigh of a cello: *dying*. But the sound of it is the only beautiful thing about it.

Several times a week I must be cleaned. Water comes to me on a sponge. I must lift my arms, shift my heels, lower my flaming eyes. I must smell pink, antiseptic. I'm removed from my place while the bed sheets are changed and set to sag in a wheelchair. I am proffered a pan, and the sight of it shames me; at other times I can't call for it fast enough. My food comes mashed, raised on a spoon; spillage will dapple my lap. I am addressed as if an idiot, cooed over as though a child. I'm woken when I wish to sleep, told to sleep when I'd prefer to be awake. I am poked, prodded, pinched, and flensed; I'm needled and wheedled and cajoled. My existence is nothing but a series of humiliations; what little life is left to me can hardly be called my own. All of this, this horror, just to say, "He's dying."

I hear the words blow like dust through town. From where I lie, in this lean white room, I hear them spoken under awnings, murmured over counters, delivered as knowing statements across gates. *It won't be long now. They say he's dying.*

They say he's fragile, his skin sugar-white; they say he must be handled like a delicate crown of thorns. They're saying he's as weightless as the skeleton of a crow.

Breathing is an undertaking: it takes minutes to sigh. My rib cage is the hull of a wrecked and submerged ship. My arms, thin as adders, are leaden as dropped boughs. The mattress, my closest friend, has been carved by the knots of my unfleshed bones into a landscape of dents. The soul might rise, but the body pulls down, accepting the inevitable, returning to where it began.

This is where I began: I am dying in my childhood home. Beyond the window straggles the only world I know and wish to know; I was born and grew up in this few-thousand town. There is nothing about its weft and fold that isn't familiar to me. I know the cracks in the footpaths — I have stepped on them a thousand times. I know the product on the shelves and the reflection in the glass — I have seen myself there, left imprints of my hands. I've felt summer's sahara heat and seen autumn's bedraggled blooms; I've kicked black crickets from my toes and fed wood to a hissing fire. I know which gate tilts in the wind; I know what's cropped in which field. I have known the exact moment when every calf and child was born. From here, on the bed, where I see only paneled walls and a haze of curtain that ushers in the breeze, I can distinguish and put a name to every rooster's cry. The breeze brings to me the scent of sawdust, diesel, feathers, chicken soup. They say that smell is the last thing to fade, so I sniff about while I can.

It is as easy for me to die here, in the bedroom of my childhood home, as it would be to die anywhere. The procession of needlers and pinchers knows where to find me. The word on the street agrees, says, "It's better he's home — it's comforting there." My aunt takes care of me from day to day; she sleeps in the neighboring room. I'll not pretend her task is enviable. The chronically ill make for difficult work; neither is it easy to be chronically ill. It is an effort for me to do anything — to think, talk, imagine, prepare — to do anything except concede to the demands of my squalling usurper. It rules me like a dictator; in turn I rule my aunt. When the end comes, Sarah will have earned her peace. In the meantime, she's not the sort to put a pillow to one's face: when the illness is looking elsewhere

I apologize for the grief I cause and, "Gabriel," she replies, "I'll miss you."

Inside me roils a thunderstorm. When I breathe, the breath is winter. Lightning jags through my chest, splashes shocks of blood down my chin. Rain falls inside my lungs, sloshes when I move. The thunder rolls like a great cat, settles with a feline weight. The marrow in my bones is ice. My eyes are hailstones.

And I feel old, as old as the mountains that the walls and window won't allow me to see, as old as if every moment has somehow stretched into a year. And anyone who didn't know me might mistake me for an ancient man — I have an old tranquility. But I am young — I'm the martyr's age. At my age, hearts are pierced with arrows, and taped over with bombs. Mine is the saintly age, the sacrificial one: I am only twenty.

But there's no one here who doesn't know me.

In this small town, conversation is whispered. Treetops, when they buffet, do so mutedly. Cats don't purr; goats don't bleat; birds keep their tunes to themselves. The cow separated from her calf swallows back her moan. Children in their yards don't play, trucks take the long road round. Anything daring to slam with the wind is forcibly nailed down. The wind itself does its best to skulk

4

unheard. Everything here is silenced, for me. Everything keeps a respectful hush. I lie alone in this small room, my childhood's unreliable sanctuary now my prison, soon my morgue, and silence, which is what awaits me, is what I've already received.

Fortunately my ears are sharp.

I hear that they are whispering, "What was missing is found."

FINNIGAN

The wind told me it's found.

I jump from my tree (they are all my trees) and click
for Surrender and breach the hill, him running in the lead.
Surrender has heavy bones, heavy ears, a timber tail, a gate-
post skull, but he's light as butter on his feet: he runs back
and forth, up and down, flushing birds that flew off yesterday, chasing rabbits that are stew. I don't call him, he
won't come. I'm going to a place that's hidden, and though
if anyone saw the dog they'd know I was near, Surrender
won't be seen.

The fact that it's found is at my shoulders like a swarm,
pushing me through the slop and fug, up and up the
mountain. The earth I touch with my hands is cold (the
earth is mine, the dirt, the seeds, the grass, the worms,
the cracks, the clods, all of it, all). The mud makes cakes
on my knees. Up high the breeze is colder, and smells like
a snake's belly, and bites with a snake's fangs. I clamber

higher, to the top. I need the peak, the view. I need the world caught inside the black pit of my eyes.

I know where I'm going, the dip in the ground, the log and mucky gouge. Before me there's been fox and wombat, and the earth tangs of them. I sit in the gouge with my arms round my knees and stare, a gargoyle on the mountain's side. If I had wings they would be black: they would unfold with a creak like antique hide and, unfolded, drip oil.

From this towersome height this is what I see: miniature town, miniature trees, a world that's a toy box upturned. A mansion for dollies, trucks driven by fleas. Then there's bigger, other things, although farther away. Forests, fields, mountains, clouds. Mountains like shark teeth, ivory, serrated; forest dense as moss. All this in my eye. Beyond this, nothing. There is no place beyond this. From here I'll see whatever comes, and I will see it before it sees I.

My hair blows in my eyes. I scrape it out with a nail.

Surrender returns, thinks, thinks about biting. His lip crooks like a wave. The one thing important to everything is this: my hound.

Another thing I see: the cemetery. Every town must have one: Mulyan has one too. No one lives forever (who'd let them?). In the cemetery everyone's related, and not just because of the state they're in. There's daughters, uncles, grandparents, fathers, sons, cousins, mothers, brothers, the same names again again again. The clans gather together like it's Christmas under there. Some had the town in themselves — *Sacred to the Memory of John Mulyan Devine*. Now it's the town that has them; now they're dust, dirt, loam. Rabbits have dug tunnels through John Devine, his rib cage a nursery for kits.

Another thing about Mulyan: nobody chooses to come here. In this little town ringed by shark-tooth mountains we are far, far away. We know only each other. And the names on the gravestones stay the same.

Mulyan hangs, upturned in my eye; a town of abominable secrets and myth. Its elders gather in the Chamber to vote against everything. They are frightened of change, and defiant. "We are happy as we are!" They are pigheaded to a person. "We'll keep our own ways, thank you!"

I full-heartedly concur. Why wouldn't I? I am the ruler of this island-town. I'm happy as things are.

The wind's chilled me as blue as a corpse; my jaw is sore, my lips skinned. From my perch I oversee the yawning town, see it waking and greeting the dawn. I rub my hands; I breathe on them; I snuggle into the earth. I watch the tip-grubber's truck grind its way to the dump. On the tray of the truck lurch twelve scrawny mutts, each salvaged from the rubble of the dump, each bearing an apostle's name. I watch the tip-grubber to the end of the road, then jump back a mile to Mulyan. Surrender wanders near. He sniffs my face; his coat is chill. I settle like a hawk.

McIllwraith the local law steps from his matchbox house. I lean forward to follow. He climbs into his minuscule car and leaves the gutter for the street. The car bucks and snorts with the cold, fog bleeding from its rear. I imagine him in the driver's seat, smiling smoothly to himself. The grave is found: it must mean good things for him. It might mean freedom, escape. He's been caged in Mulyan for years. Now the grave is open; maybe so is a door. Maybe now, at long last, someone will recognize a job well done.

A job well done, like a kiss.

I unfold into the wind. I whistle Surrender from the mountain's spine. He runs and pinecones tumble in his wake, but there isn't any hurry. In the grave they'll have found only bones, and bones don't require hurry. "Surrender," I say. "Surrender."

GABRIEL

What they have found will be bone, because it's been a long time. Femur, fibula, tibia, humerus; clavicle, mandible, scapula, vertebrae. Tiny little phalanges gnawed on by a rat. Animal becomes vegetable becomes mineral and it happens quickly, but everything mineral knows how to wait. Bones have the patience of the moon.

Now that they have been found, Finnigan will start to move. Wherever he's been holed up will suddenly feel precarious to him. If he is smart he will resist the urge to leave a trail of destruction behind him. There is nothing like a burning bush to cast light upon your face. And Finnigan is far from stupid—he is sharp as a trap. His cleverness has been his saving grace, and mine. Finnigan roams unhindered through the valley and town, the midnight raider of kitchens, the sleeper-in-woolsheds, the bareback horse-rider, the bather in rushing streams. He is dirt under fingernails and the stick of sap on skin. This clean wan bed is my citadel, this room my continent. My powdered skin is silken, tinted airless-blue. If you touch me I will bruise; if I shift, to ease my weight, blood rivers from my nose. I am saintly, poetic; I am demise, other-world. But when Finnigan runs, I run with him.

I am Gabriel, the messenger, the teller of astonishing truths. Now I am dying, my temperature soaring, my hands and memory tremoring: perhaps I should not be held accountable for everything I say.

I remember my first sight of him—the sound and scavenger look of him—surrounded by summer; I remember the stillness of the day and the density of the air. Neither of us was older than nine or ten. I was skimming a car along the garden fence when Finnigan crossed the brink of my vision. At first I feigned ignorance or disdain of his presence, but the car beneath my fingertips bunny-hopped and soon stalled. I slid a glance at him. At school we had seen a wildlife film projected onto a wall, and the boy who was watching me was a hyena. His dark eyes were set apart and seemed to have no arena of white. He didn't move or say a thing but I knew, just from his watching, that he could sever my arm. We were the same height and same age and built along similar leggy lines, but he was a hyena while I was a small, ashy, alpine moth. From the footpath side of the fence he stared at me, and my gaze floated grudgingly from the toy. He swiped a fly from his face. "You're that boy," he said.

". . . What boy?"

"You know. That boy. You know. What you did. Everybody knows."

I pressed my thumb on the bonnet of the car. I looked my interrogator up and down. His clothes were shabby and ill-fitting. The fly had returned to his face. "You're the kook boy," he elaborated, conversationally. "Your mother and father are kooks, too. Everybody knows."

I considered the situation, his evident supremacy. Diplomatically, I laughed. "Kooks," I said, and found it a sweet word, confectionery. I hopped illustratively from one foot to the other, waggling my head. The boy smiled; I saw myself jumping inside his lush eyes. "Kooks," I chirruped again, to prove I'd taken no offense.

He leaned on the pickets; his gaze dipped to the car and away. "Your mother is a witch," he said. "Everybody knows."

There seemed no response required to this so I smiled and, suddenly inspired, pretended my knee itched, and attended to scratching it. The gypsy boy watched silently, the fly sniffing the corner of his mouth. I stamped my foot

on the soft garden earth. The wind shifted shadows on our
hands. I had never seen this boy before, and was honored
that a stranger should have given my family such thought.
I didn't want him to go away. I asked, "How come you don't
go to school?"

"Why would I?" he replied.

His eyes returned to the car parked on the fence
railing. I poked it so it rattled forward over the terrain.
My father's sister Sarah had sent the car in the mail,
my name printed clearly on the gray cardboard box. The
plaything had so far managed to escape my mother's ruth-
less confiscation. The visitor's eyes lingered on the car
until I felt a twitch of nerves — then, mercifully, his gaze
moved on, traveling the walls of the house. The wind
rolled, scattering dust; I smelled the paint on the fence,
the heat in the leaves, the parched conclusion of the
afternoon. The boy, so close, smelled of nothing. He
slipped a fist between the pickets and asked, "What do I
have in my hand?"

I looked at the fist curled under my nose, the wrist
lightly touching the rail. His fingers were brown as the
legs of a huntsman, the skin on the knuckles broken. In
my mind's eye I pictured what such fingers could hide. A
tooth, a stone, a beetle. "Money?"

He smiled. "You cheated." His fingers unfurled; there lay three damp coins. I had never seen such riches in the palm of a boy. "Where did you get it?" I asked.

"Took it from Mother's purse." His smile grew.

"Won't she find out? You'll get in trouble."

"She won't find out. Not unless you tell."

"I won't." I would always do whatever he wanted. "What will you do with it?"

He shrugged; his gaze again brushed the car. He looked too poor to own toys or to have an aunt who could send them. My heart was gripped with sudden horror. "This is mine!" I squeaked.

The boy stared evenly at me; then the tawny lips bent in scorn. "Why would I want it?" he asked.

My face drenched scarlet, I glanced away. In that moment I hated the car, hated my aunt for giving it to me, felt painful pity for them both. I scooped up the toy gently, as if it were injured, and slipped it between the buttons of my shirt. I knew I would never play with it again. The dark boy watched in silence, slouched against the fence. After a time he said, "Come out into the street."

I shook my head unhappily, unable to look at him. "I'm not allowed. I have to stay in the yard."

The boy pinched the fence with his toes. "That's a kook thing."

"On Saturdays I can play in the street."

My voice was hitched—somewhere there were tears. The boy considered me while the wind flipped his hair. The road had stayed empty for such a long time. "What day is today?"

I glanced up, surprised. "Don't you know?"

"Why should I?"

His lack of shame was awesome. "It's Thursday."

"Every day's the same to me."

"Come back on Saturday." I shifted closer. "Not tomorrow, the next day."

I watched him intently, beggingly, felt I'd fall down if he refused. I knew I couldn't bring him into the house, that I shouldn't mention him to my mother or father, but I longed to have his promise, I hungered for the prospect of him. If my visitor walked away now he would seem like a daydream, like touching a tiger's face in the dark. And my visitor seemed indifferent to the proposal, continuing to pinch the fence with his toes. He opened his fist, which still rested on the rail, and checked that the coins remained there. Unexpectedly he said, "Do us a favor?"

"Yes, I will! What?"

"Hide this money in your pocket."

I shied away, gormless. "How come?"

"No pockets." He slapped his trousers. "Just until Saturday."

My throat went dry. Stealing from a purse was a crime with which I did not wish to be associated. "If your mother won't know you took it," I said, "why do you need me to hide it?"

The boy considered me coolly, then, disgusted, turned away. "Wait!" I yipped. He stopped, and stood there saying nothing while I flailed with my conscience. I desperately wanted to befriend this gypsy, but he would not return without reason. He would have no use for a friend who lacked a spirit as robust as his own. I pressed to the fence, my voice husky: "What would I do with it?"

"Bury it?"

"But—couldn't you?"

He snorted. "If *I* hide it, it won't be hidden, will it?"

I gulped and meekly shuffled as he dropped the coins in my shirt pocket, where they beat like a steely heart. He cocked his head to study me, and seemed satisfied. "Give them back on Saturday. Don't tell anyone."

I nodded breathlessly. "What's your name?"

A cat's smile touched his lips. I hung on the fence while he scouted in the gutter until he found a weathered piece of glass, which he held up ceremoniously to my gaze. He nudged my hands aside, and I watched with quickening disquiet as he applied the point of the glass to the thick paint on the fence rail. A hundred protests shrieked in my mind as he carefully carved one letter after another, and frail spirals of waxy paint curled away from the blade and blew off in the breeze. I dredged my voice from the depths: "Stop!" I gasped. "Don't do that!"

"It's finished now," he said, as if the offense, completed, was somehow lessened. He wiped a palm across what he'd written and I leaned closer to look. He had carved a long word in a somersault language that seemed oddly familiar to me:

When I glanced up, he was watching me, an oily shine in his eyes. In them I saw the reflection of the house behind me, the crimson windows and door frame, the anorexic tangle of roses planted against the weatherboard.

"Anwell!"

I jumped, my heart skidding. I turned to see my mother standing at the flywire screen. Finnigan vanished instantly leaving no trace behind. "Inside," my mother ordered. "Come inside."

I come back to my room as if thrown into it. Inside my lungs the thunderstorm clashes, spliced by lightning. Coughing rakes my lungs, strains the cartilage between my bones. Blood splatters my chin and chest, warm, thick as cream. I hunch under the agony, pillows tumbling down my back, and across the chalk-white cotton sheets the ruby stains anchor, disperse, extend.

Then Sarah is beside me, holding the cloth to my lips, her strong hands circling my breaking spine. Like sailors on a raging sea, neither of us can do anything but wait until the storm is done. Sarah smooths my hair, murmurs words, lets me know I'm not alone. Tears slip to my chin but I'm not overcome, they mean nothing, they are simply a symptom.

Not yet, I'm thinking, not yet. I will, and soon, I promise, but not yet. Give me just a little more time: when she's come and gone, I'll go.

And it pleases itself to give me a little more time.

I do not look too closely at the cloth with which Sarah wipes my chest. Nothing sears the eyes more deeply than the sight of one's own blood on cloth. She brings a glass of water and helps me drink from it: I swallow the blood that's coated my teeth and the taste of dying swills away. The pain fades, my lungs fill, and the illness retreats good-naturedly — as if all this time it's just been playing, as if all this has just been a joke.

There is blood on my nightshirt, its outline like a continent, detailed at the edges. The article is removed and discarded, as is the blemished sheet. The clean nightshirt my aunt drapes over me is freezing against my skin. I am shivering, stupefied.

Sarah asks me if I need the pan. I tell her to leave me alone. A house call from the illness always leaves me morose. I bury myself in blankets, into a dark private place. Inside my lungs, air is probing passages that are suddenly unblocked; other routes are newly closed, clogged with the debris of the storm. Every time the illness wreaks havoc, it leaves a few more passages irreversibly barricaded. I am suffocating.

When I close my eyes I see Finnigan as plainly as if he were beside me.

My mother discovered the coins almost immediately — I had no talent for secrecy then. The few sad coins she fished from my pocket looked like teardrops or bullet holes in her palm. She held them close to her nose, stared at them, nostrils flaring; I stood gazing at the bony flank of her hand. She wore a bruising diamond ring on her wedding finger. She sniffed sharply, her lip jerked. "Where did you get this?" she asked.

I could not say. The hallway of our house was long and always cold; the exit doors, back and front, were kept frowningly closed. The warmth of outside was shaved from my skin and fell in curls to the floor.

"Anwell? Answer me. Where did you get this?"

She was staring over her fingers at me, her face lean as a goat's. I looked away, because I could never meet her eye. My gaze ran like a fearful mouse along the skirting board and up the wall. A field of pink rosebuds was wallpapered flatly there. My mother cuffed me to attention. "Anwell!"

Dizziness wobbled through me. I said, "I can't say."

Mother gazed at me, her face a tomb, her body a pole. "Did you steal them?"

"No—"

"Did you take them from my purse? From your father's wallet? My God—from someone on the street?"

"No!"

She grabbed my wrist like a snare grabs a fox. I jumped backward, a snared fox, and her grip tightened. Her body piked down so her eyes were at mine. "Because you know you are a thief," she said. "This whole town knows what you are. They whisper about you. *Look at the little beast. What a burden for his poor mother.* Look at me, with your lying face, and tell me the truth!"

"I didn't steal it." Fear sang like violins. "I swear—"

She wasn't listening. Her fingers crushed my wrist. "You want to make a fool of your mother. You want your mother to die of shame. You want to kill your mother."

"No!" I yelped, and struggled madly, leaping like a fox. "I don't—I didn't!"

"Then *where* did you get it, Anwell? Answer me!"

I pressed my lips together; I would not tell a lie. My mother, staring into my face, made a sound like a dog or a bird. Clutching my wrist she rushed me down the hall, bursting into her bedroom like a gale. Her black bead handbag lay on the bed and from its maw Mother pulled her purse, twisting its clip as if breaking bones. I retreated stumblingly, till my shoulders knocked the wall. Rosebuds cascaded from the ceiling to the floor. Mother stared with satisfaction into the purse, her skull pressed hard against the flesh, her throat swallowing sourly. She looked at me, her face crumpling. "How could you?" Her eyes like axes. "How could you?"

I caught my breath. "Mama, I—"

"You terrible creature. How could you?"

GABRIEL

Tears dashed down my cheeks, each one quicker than the last. I leaned against the wall and sobbed, struggling to swallow back the terror because she hated tears, they enraged her. She lowered her shattered self to the bed, crumpling the purse in her hand. She gazed at the wall, white-eyed. "All the dreadful things you've done," she whispered, from somewhere in the clouds.

I stood miserably beside the wall, a thread of tears making the short plunge from my chin to the floor. I longed to beg her forgiveness, but my voice would not come. The icebox odor of my mother's bedroom made my empty stomach clench. My socks were bunched inside my shoes, my tears greasing the floor. I still had the toy car hidden in my shirt. A disjoined part of me fretted over the loss of Finnigan's coins, and worried about what he would say.

My mother finally looked at me. "Look what you do to poor Mother," she sighed.

I licked my salty lips. "I'm sorry."

"You know I must tell Father."

"But I didn't—"

"Anwell," she said, "I despise you when you lie."

We were both quiet. The afternoon light was netted by the lace curtains; no color came into this room. "Maybe you don't have to tell him," I suggested.

"I won't be a liar like you."

So we waited, me with my shoulders to the cool rosebud wall, and she, upright as a churchgoer, propped on the end of the bed. I kept my thoughts anchored on the word carved into the fence.

FINNIGAN

Me and Surrender fishhook round the town. Already it's darker, though it isn't noon. I can smell snow on peaks miles from here. The sun's like a coin that's been buried for years. As we walk, warts of moss sprout. The footpath is covered with wet, grisly leaves. The wind blows at my back, drives eucalypt bark clattering into the gutter. It sings to us a triumphal song. All the world is a stage, for me and Surrender.

And it's cold cold cold; in winter you would never guess that Mulyan burns so well.

I know all that goes on in the houses we pass. I tell Surrender about it as we trundle along. Everything here belongs to me: I reign; I infect this town. I'm the unexplained noises, each mislaid bit and piece. I'm the murmur, the shadow, the creaking floor. I'm the blackout, the echo, the scratcher-at-the-door.

In this fibro shanty lives Mr. Rich, who gives what he has to the poor. Down the lane from him lives Mr. Pomfrey, who went blind during the war. Over the way, there's Mr. Sinjay, who can hear like any canine; upstairs from him is Ms. Silvestri, who dabbles in the Black Arts. Mr. Hall dines alone since his wife became famous and took her own life; Mrs. Click has teeth of shoddy fit and ignores the blemish that's bloomed on her skin. Oh it's cold, cold. Miss Tucker has filthy habits that are best not spoken of; Mr. Lee's a closet quiffer, and so's his wife and son. Mr. Darling, from number five, collects women's magazines; behind that fence lives Mr. Pye, otherwise known as the Human Sludge. Miss Hooper, who lives alone, curls into her pillows at night and cries because her life is stillborn; Mr. Mead, two doors away, has three grown daughters and an adoring wife, but he sits in his potting shed most afternoons and quietly weeps at the wall. There's no pleasing some people.

I've touched them all: I'm like the plague. I've shared a bed with the best of them; I've shared their finest meals. I've listened to their rumors and the sounds they make at night. I have stood beside their children's cribs while they sucked their thumbs and dreamed. Tonight I'll share the schoolteacher's fire, having hissed the resident vixen from her place beneath the floor. Before dawn tomorrow I'll have drawn a wet lamb into the world and have dragged its fat cousin away. The icing on the bakery's buns will preserve, come morning, the imprint of my fingers. Surrender and I eat well.

Before then, though, there's a few things to do. See the bones for myself. Grace McIllwraith with my presence. Pay a long-time-coming visit to that dying creature on a bed.

GABRIEL

I remember how keen I was to assure him it wasn't his fault, that I didn't blame him for the scarlet welts striping the back of my knees; I remember how my skin prickled to see him, how I flew to the fence at the sight of him swaggering along the street, unkempt and unshod as he'd been two days earlier, leggy as a jackal. I had feared and feared he wouldn't come, had traced his name with my fingertips hoping to cast a returning spell. I had chewed my nails to the quick.

When I confessed to him the loss of the coins, Finnigan wasn't angry. "Show us your knees," he said, and leaned past the pickets to inspect what remained of the thrashing. We stood in the shade of the ash that grew by the roadside and overhung our garden and peppered the lawn, each spring, with arrowheads, to my father's horticultural ire. Clutching a handful of shrubbery, I hoisted my trousers and showed him the marks on my knees. Finnigan squinted and smiled. "Hurt?"

"Mmm."

"What'd he use? Belt?"

"Feather-duster. The stick. The handle."

My visitor whistled. "Quick or slow?"

I reflected. "Quick."

"Quick stings but it's finished faster."

Mulyan boys were whipped routinely and made comrades of each other in the comparing of war wounds, but I knew my parents wouldn't approve of me profiting from my punishment this way. I smoothed my trousers down. "I'm sorry about the money."

Finnigan shrugged, and I understood that he thought himself fairly, even pleasingly, compensated by my pain. The shade moved among hanks of his hair. I noticed, when he stood straight, that he was exactly as tall as me. "Let's go to the cattle yards."

I shook my head regretfully. My mother was taking her afternoon nap, her curtain drawn against the heat and light; my father was in his study, where he passed hours over petals pressed and tagged and dried. This time I was safest, and yet I never felt safe. "I have to stay where I can be seen."

His eyes scanned my face. "Kooksville."

"I can sit on the footpath—"

"Kooks," he said chillingly. "That's what everyone says you are, and that's what you are."

I pleaded for understanding. "Mother won't let me—"

"Don't ask her." He smiled gamely. "Then she can't say no."

"But . . . I'll get thrashed."

"You're a kook *and* a chicken."

"No!" I squawked. "Don't say that!"

"Why not? Only a *baby* does what he's told."

I gawped at him, shattered. Leaves tumbled along the path, pushed by the parched north wind. The leaves scratched past Finnigan, flickered and clickered away. I clutched my fingers in despair. He wouldn't waste time on someone tethered, like me—already I could feel him drift. I prayed for salvation to fall from the sky. Finnigan picked a scab and studied the bauble of blood. He glanced at me with his predator's eyes. "Sometimes you get a thrashing even when you try to be *good*."

I caught a breath—until I heard him speak those words, I'd never known that other boys also suffered in this way, that *every* boy feels he has some mischief owed to him, restitution for the times he's been punished without

29

fair cause. I went to the gate slid the bolt stepped over to the other side, before I could change my mind.

The cattle yards sprawled over a distant corner of the town and we walked through the sunburned streets without talking, me giddy with excitement, Finnigan dragging a broken stick. Shadows made the footpath black then white, black then white. Distantly we heard cheering as a bail tumbled from its perch. Dogs barked as we passed their gates, rabble-rousing the canine town. Tea towels draped on veranda rails blew horizontal on the wind. The applause of a TV audience rode the stuffy air. We passed no one, and I was relieved. Each footstep carried me away.

The cattle yards were deserted, for this was not a sale day. We slipped between strings of rusty wire and only sun skinks watched us weave our way between the post-and-rail pens; a king snake slid shyly behind corrugated iron and seven ravens flapped away. Cattle ghosts were there, though, in the rich fawn scent of their hide, in hair snagged on fence palings and hoofprints preserved in hard mud. There was no sadder sound in Mulyan than the moaning of the cows, which, every other month or so, were crowded into these yards, smacked and spooked and harried and jostled, and offered up for sale.

Separated from their companions and calves, they would call chestily to each other until the mountains reverberated with their sighs.

That afternoon I followed Finnigan with humble adoration, astonished that this boy who was as wild as a hawk should look so kindly upon me. We poked around the loading ramps where countless Christmas beetles dangled from spider webs, their brilliant carapaces flaring in the sun. We climbed the iron ladder to the top of the great gray tank and stared solemnly into the water at quaking images of ourselves. We hung our weight from butcher's chains and raced in circles until our feet lifted from the grassless ground. Finnigan found a severed calf's tail, and flies came off it like rain. His walk was confident as a rooster's and although he rarely looked at me and hardly spoke at all, I sensed that he had not forgotten my presence, that he was guarded as a dog with a bone. We crouched in the shade of a corrugated roof and watched ants mill over the corpse of a skink. "Where do you come from?" I dared to ask him. "Where's your home?"

He waved a wrist to somewhere distant. "Over there. The hills."

"Do you have a family?"

"A mother and father. Like you."

"And brothers or sisters?"

He found a twig and touched the skink and the ants ran haywire. He looked at me, his chin on his shoulder. "No." A whiff of danger rose from him; I saw the hyena again. "What about you?" he asked. "Do you have brothers or sisters?"

Some of the ants sprinted across my fingers. "No."

" . . . But you used to. You had a brother."

I said, "I don't want to talk about that."

"What was his name?"

The subject always filled me with something like tar. The word stuck inside like a splinter, had to be drawn out of me. "Vernon," I muttered. "I can't talk about it."

He let a moment pass, pondering. "Do you think about him? Do you remember what you did?"

I stared fretfully at my interrogator, flies seesawing in front of my eyes. "I'm not supposed to talk about it. My mother says."

"Baby. Chicken. She's not here."

There was nothing for it but to answer. "Sometimes he's in my dreams. That's all."

"And you remember what you did."

"Hmm."

"A bad thing."

I screwed my face up, pained. "I was only seven. You don't know any better, when you're only seven."

"But it was bad. And you're sorry."

I scratched the dust, looked askance.

"You wish you never did it, even though you were only seven."

"It was an accident!" I barked.

"I know," said Finnigan.

I blinked in surprise at this, and suddenly liked him more. He looked away, watching the ants collect themselves and find their way back to the skink. His frayed clothes did not fit or suit him, seemed stolen or handed down; his brown skin was made browner by its lacquer of earth. His ears were specked with sand, like seashells, his face and arms ocher with grime. On his chin was a scuffed green stain, from falling hard in the grass. I guessed he was a farm boy, which was something town boys like myself despised as a dirty and ignorant thing to be. Yet Finnigan's dirt seemed good dirt, like the dirt on a running dog's paws, and I sensed he knew much — possibly everything. Maybe not spelling, maybe not the days of the week, but everything that a hawk might know, everything worth knowing. A dullard I had never been, but in the presence of this gypsy boy I knew my head to be an empty bucket, my brain a waterlogged sock. I put it to him: "How come you know so much, when you don't even go to school?"

"You go to school," he answered, "but you don't know anything."

His cleverness sprang a smile to my face, I shuffled a little closer. "Don't your mother and father *make* you go to school?"

"Nope." Finnigan's nose was at the corpse. "They don't know what I do."

I marveled at the idea, a life of secrets and decisions. "Don't you even *want* to go?"

He prodded the reptile with a bitten nail, and the ants fanned out in panic. "What's so good about school? *You* don't like it. Everyone there reckons you're kooksville. No one is your friend."

I felt my face redden under its skin of sunburn. "If you went to school," I said, "*you* could be my friend. We could be each other's friend. If I told someone about you, how you want to go to school — maybe they would let you. My father is a lawyer, everyone listens to him. Maybe, if I asked him, he could — "

Like a spider Finnigan jumped at me, slamming me head over heels. Dust wallowed around us, clouding the hot air. The wild boy's eyes were close to mine, his dirty muzzle and teeth. Hanks of my shirt were crushed in his hands. "Who hit you?" he yelled. "Who hurt you?"

I remembered the sear of the feather-duster's handle, but it was Finnigan who terrified me: "I won't!" I wailed. "I won't tell!"

"You better *not!*"

"No, no, I won't—"

"Because if you *do*, I'll never talk to you! I'll *never* visit you! You can just be a kook by yourself!"

He released my shirt and I scrambled aside, huddling against the fence. Finnigan swung away and stalked the yard, kicking up clouds of dust. "They'd break me into pieces," he was saying to himself. "Here a piece, here a piece." I sniveled and wiped tears from my eyes. I seemed doomed to infuriate those people I most wanted to please, and I cursed and hated myself.

He spun suddenly to face me, and I cringed under his gaze. "No one would believe you," he said flatly.

I sniffed and nodded; Finnigan gazed at me. "No one would believe you," he reiterated. "And I would maybe kill you."

I drew a throttled breath. "I won't tell. I promise. I'll keep you a secret."

Finnigan considered this, glowing gold in the afternoon sun. I said nothing and dared not move. A flock of cockatoos passed over the yards, high in the sea-blue sky. "A secret," the wild boy said finally, and his tense shoulders fell. "You keep me like a secret."

He sat beside me in the boxy shade of the fence, resting his wrists on his knees. For a while we said nothing. I was still nervous and ashamed. Finnigan coughed dustily, and brushed ants off his toes. The corrugated iron creaked with the heat; in the shady center of the corral a bush fly flew round and round. Finnigan said, "Whew, it's hot."

I nodded loosely. He looked at me.

"You must feel pretty bad about your brother."

I nodded again, wonky as a doll.

"You must wish you never did such a bad thing."

I sighed. "Yeah."

"We should make—a *packet*, or something." He struggled. "A packet. You swear not to do bad things—never again. From now on, you only do good things."

I smiled uncertainly, sunburn tight on my nose. "I don't think that's possible."

"Why not? That's what you wish, isn't it?"

"Yeah, but everyone does bad things sometimes, you can't help it."

"I can help it," said Finnigan. "I'll do the bad things for you. Then you won't have to. You can just do good things."

I stared at him, mystified. "A bit like cops-and-robbers, you mean?"

"Yeah!" His eyes brightened. "You would be an angel! Your mother and father would be happy, if you were like an angel!"

This was true—I imagined my parents would very much relish having an angel for a son. Who, after all, would not? Still, I didn't like the idea. There was something soul-selling about it: somewhere in its gluey depths, there was a trick concealed. "But what about you?" I asked. "You'd be in trouble all the time."

He answered with confidence, "I wouldn't. If I was doing your bad things for you, you'd owe me. You couldn't let me get caught. You would have to hide me. You'd have to sneak things out for me to eat. You'd have to tell lies, to cover my tracks."

"But lying is a *bad* thing."

"Not when you're lying for me. That wouldn't count. That would be part of the packet."

I nodded doubtfully; I did not say "pact."

"You will only be *good* things—you'll never get angry or fight. And I will only be *bad* things—I will always get

37

angry and fight. We'll be like opposites—like pictures in the water—"

"Reflections, you mean?"

"Yeah, reflections! The same, but different. Like twins—like blood brothers! And when you need something bad done, like punishment or revenge, you'll just ask me, and I will do it—"

"And when you need something *good* done, you'll just ask me?"

He hesitated, as if doubting such a need would arise. "Uh-huh."

I thought on this. I did not tell him I'd always considered cops-and-robbers an idiot's game. I asked, "How would I find you, if I needed you? I'm not allowed out the front gate."

This flaw in the plan did not faze him. "If you do what I say, you could always find me. I'd be in the trees and under the house or in the coop or on the roof. I'd always be somewhere nearby, I swear. I'd be your best friend."

I bit my lip and glanced away. Those magical words made my eyes water, so friendless was I. I knew that I'd agree to anything that would catch his loyalty and cage him. I said, "You'd have to be careful. Mother wouldn't like it, if she saw you on the roof."

He laughed. "She'd never see me. I wouldn't let anyone see me—only you."

His flattery made me smile. I leaned against the spiny yard-post, keeping myself in the shade. My head vaguely hurt. I couldn't understand how Finnigan had conjured this odd notion, nor what he could do with my promise to comply; I had a strange sense that he'd arranged all this—the coins, the loss of them, the writing on the fence rail, the gritty, flyblown yards—simply to bring us to this moment, to seal this agreement with me. But I thought about what he was offering—friendship to the friendless, protection to the vulnerable, courage for the weak—and it seemed such a small thing, to exchange a word for this. I thought about a life lived in shimmering goodness and wondered if this wasn't, in fact, the path of repentance, if this was not the truest way of making amends. I looked into his clever face and said, "All right."

Finnigan kicked with delight, his heels exploding the dust. "Should we swear it?"

I laughed, he was so happy. "How do you mean?"

"Well, we should cut ourselves, or something."

I faltered. "Better not."

So Finnigan cut his own skin, having scouted up a splinter sharp enough to pierce his thumb, and I watched as he dug out a seam of blood without flinching and smeared it first across his forehead, then across my own. In a hushed voice he asked me, "What's an angel's name?"

Back then I had never heard of Raphael, Zadkiel, Jophiel, Uriel—I knew only the most famous, the mysterious visitor. "Gabriel," I suggested, and Finnigan approved.

Gabriel. The blood on my forehead crimped and itched when it dried. I would always be lonely, but no more alone.

My condition has deteriorated to such a state that Sarah thought it best to call the doctor. He arrives big as a bullock, ungainly in this small tidy room; he is full of joviality and newsy tidbits, scolds me lightly for inching closer to the grave. His visits exhaust me—I think I actually hate him. His yellow smile—all of him is yellow—patrols the room like a lighthouse beam, falling on my sandy-beach aunt, on jagged-rocky-outcrop me, on the foaming blankets of the sea, but when he bends his head to commune with my pulse, his smile dims. He puts a paw against my wrist, checks the whites of my eyes. He sticks a thermometer under my tongue and fondles the glands in my throat. He is attempting to talk to the illness, to weasel into its confidence. He hopes to win its trust so it might, for a moment, drop its guard. But the sickness won't be drawn out by anyone, and treats my yellow doctor with contempt. It is not in the business of folding, but of raising the stakes.

He knows it, and in his muffled smile I see my future. Still, part of me is proud to be dying such a tricksy death.

"He's restless," says Sarah. "He kicks off the blankets."

"Tuck them in tight," prescribes the doctor. "It's cold outside. You've heard the news, of course. And what they've found."

"Yes." Sarah speaks quietly. "I haven't said anything to him."

I lie in silence like idiot-child, listening to them make a matter of me as if I were not in the room. And indeed my temperature has spiked so high that in some ways I *have* left the room, left the house, left time behind. In some way I still sit with Finnigan in the angled shadows of the saleyard, our lean limbs stretched like flies' legs, his blood tight on my skin.

Once I'd given my promise I couldn't take it back: indeed, once the word passed my lips I felt I'd met a moment that had always been waiting for me, that I'd taken a place in which my name was long carved. I understood that this was fate, and that I was fated. In surrendering my right to do wrong I forfeited great chunks of free will, but I have managed without it. It's true that I, in common with many called on to be saintly, initially viewed my calling with dismay; the prospect of a pious life made me queasy even as Finnigan sucked the blood from his thumb. But I have never gone back on my word; I have kept my side of the packet, as Finnigan has always kept his. I do not think we have ever been a disappointment to each other. We have been, as he hoped, like reflections, twins.

FINNIGAN

Me and Surrender go into the forest.

Surrender is a big lazy loping hound with a tail that curves like a scythe; his coat is the color of cinnamon. His head is hefty and square as a shoebox, and he carries it slung down. His ears are each as broad as my feet, his paws as broad as my palm. When he runs, the earth trembles. When he barks, the trees bow down.

But Surrender can slink into anyone's chicken coop and pluck from her roost the fattest white hen and bring her to me without ruffling a feather or even disturbing her sleep. Good dog.

He runs through the forest (he thinks he owns it), never breaking a twig. This part of the forest is mongrel, ironbarks, which belong here, mixed with pine that never would, and now this forest is dreggy, useless, half-breed. It is not the place for picnics, it's not named on tourist maps. Only creatures come here—owls, foxes, possums, cats, rats, mice, Surrender, me. It's too shady for snakes and lizards, too close-grown for an eagle to spread his wings. This place is for the lithe and fugitive: this place is fringe.

The dog and the boy pick their way through the forest, surefooted as billy goats. The rocks are black with rotten moss but under the blackness are stripes of color, caramel, woodblood, clay, snow. Beyond the canopy the winter sun glows but down here all is gloom. The air smells clean, like spring water, cold, like a mountain's mood.

I'm looking for something, my eyes are peeled. I'm listening for something that's not a possum shifting its chunky rump. All of nature's my confederate, the weather, the soil, the creatures, the leaves, and they lead the way for me. When we come to a place where the twigs are broken and the earth is scuffed, I know we're finally here. Surrender lags as I creep forward and the ground says nothing under my weight, the ferns drape veils over me. Thanks to this I am invisible, I'm the shadow of a tree.

What I see makes my eyes smart. The ribbons they've used to map out the scene are stinging yellow and red. A blue sheet of plastic makeshifts a tent, which cracks and bucks with the breeze. The collection bags, though crystal clear, are lettered in alarm-bell orange. The digging tools they're using are silver as werewolf bullets. The colors scream so loud at me that I clap my hands to my ears.

They've been careful not to break anything. All around the pit itself, not a twig is bent. The leaf litter has been trampled only with tiptoe. The few spines of weedy grass have been combed through with gloved hands. There's been no *please* about this, though. Everything has been expected to cough up what it knows.

I'm a shadow on the edge of a cliff, and when I look down I'm looking into the pit. The pit is crude, not the shape of a grave—more the shape of something evolved overnight, like fungus on a tree. The pit is shallow, its flanks lushly dark. It's empty now, but I know what they found. The bones that escaped the mouse and the fox would have been black as the ground. Rain would have blotted them with waterstars, snails nibbled them hollow as whistles. Roots of saplings would have netted them like fish, mushrooms would've used them as bedrock. Worms curled in the cavern of a skull would have been safe from deep rain. Water, soil, bugs, slugs—these would have combined to make rags of the cloth that went with the bones to the grave.

The bones and cloth are forest now; it's theft to take them away. The wind, in protest, raises its voice. The trees, rustling, agree. Things should have been left where they were, but they weren't. Oh well.

I ease back into my shadow, having seen what I came to see. I've seen how rainwater, sheeting from the cliff, washed away enough soil to lay the bones bare. I shake my head with regret: but for this happening, they would not have been found.

I have seen, not been seen. That's a sweet way of life. I whistle Surrender like a bird, and we melt away.

GABRIEL

And then for a long time I did not see him, though I thought
about him often and looked for him in the unlikely places
he'd promised I would find him — under the house, on its
roof, in the spindly canopy of the eucalypt trees. Sitting
beneath the pines at school, watching a lunchtime game
of chase, I wished he were there beside me — I wished
he were there to run faster than my schoolfellows, to be
seen as my fleet and admirable friend. The eccentric reputation of my mother and father — a thing unavoidably
inherited by myself — protected me from obvious harm,
but as a schoolboy I was frequently the target for the
skewed cricket ball, the savagely jerked elbow, the scorn
of a farmer's son. My books would inexplicably vanish; the
girls giggled slyly at me. If I answered a teacher's question
correctly, I was mercilessly mocked in the yard; if I tried
to please by being doltish, I was tormented all the more.
By ten years old I had learned to say nothing, to keep my

head sourly down. Inside me, though, I daydreamed of the damage Finnigan could do. My enemies would flee like dogs across the hills, if only he were here. He had sworn to be near when I needed him, the living retaliation for my hurts, but he wasn't. When, at home, I committed some crime — spilled my drink, broke a plate, went cretinously deaf to what I was told — and found myself kneeling in the corner where I was traditionally sent to contemplate my sins, I remembered Finnigan's vow to protect and give me courage, and I supposed that he had lied. I might have believed I'd invented him, that I had indeed patted the tiger in the dark, had it not been for the misshapen word carved into the front fence, six small letters on which my faith hung.

And then one day, when I had turned eleven and a long droughted summer was coming to an end, a bushfire sprang to life high in the ranges and for seven legendary days it burned without mercy, skipping the roads in great leaps and bounds, striding across rivers and dams, skimming over firebreaks to rear triumphant in the oil-filled, gravel-dry forests. The sky above the valley was hooded with grease that blotted out sun and stars; the mountain peaks, miles apart, were linked by cathedrals of flame. Men fought their way up the blackened slopes as kangaroos and deer galloped down, their red hides wafting white smoke. Men fought the fire through the days and nights, although there was no night—the midnight sky was luminescent, incandescent, spangling pink, green, yellow, and orange as if the Devil had swallowed us down. The bushfire screamed an unholy hymn, its cavernous voice riding the heat waves. Women stood on verandas in the breathless evenings, staring hopelessly into the hills; the leaping, singing circle of flame glittered in their eyes. The children loitering beside their mothers were slack-mouthed and enthralled. The school was closed, the church was open. Clothes hung on clotheslines were brought in stiff as planks. The mountain farms were evacuated, the stock loosed to run for their lives.

I remember that the sound of the fire was a continual roar—I remember blocking my ears to the boom of eucalypts exploding. For seven days and seven nights, scorched leaves fell as hellish rain. I remember the air smelled of everything that had died, that birds dropped like pebbles from the smoke-raddled sky. I remember a truck with the pace of a hearse and on its tray a horror of bloated remains. I remember the farmers watching it pass and how one of them sagged in the gutter, and rested his head on his knees.

I knew, with the first brilliant flare of sparks, that this was Finnigan's work. I understood that in these months of silence he'd concentrated his abilities. The fire was Finnigan, talking to me. I hid in my room the day they started saying *arson*. I hunched beneath my bed hearing the air itself burn, praying that our friendship didn't show on my face. I prayed that, wherever he was, he was better hidden than I. Mostly I prayed, in cowardly panic, that he would stay away from me—that, if caught and interrogated, he would loyally fail to mention me.

The monstrous blaze was extinguished by a storm that first massed in the west and hung for a while, deliberating, before moving its clouds forward like battleships and dourly pouring rain. The fire leaped and darted, wounded by the drops; it changed direction and tried to escape, racing down a hill. In the face of rain the magnificent firestorm became frantic and flimsy as a fawn. The lightning clouds solemnly pursued it. Men took off their hats and let the water slick down their hair. Women on verandas laid their hands to their eyes. There was a terrible noise, the death rattle of a thousand lions. Dragon tails of soot lashed the sky. People came from their houses to witness the fire die. When the smoke and clouds and smog cleared you could see how hungry the blaze had been, how it left in its wake a crisp ebony nothingness that shone—when moonlight touched the naked hills, the blackness of them *shone*. I stood at my window and studied it night after night for a week, maybe two. Fingers of greenery sprouted across the hills then, and the sleekness of the wasteland was spoiled.

It was a month or so later that I crouched in the arbor where my father grew his most finicky roses and, sniffing ash, glanced round to see the firebug standing among the tendrils. His unheralded appearance made me catch my breath; I murmured, "Where have you been?"

He'd grown taller in his absence, but not much; his eyes were still a whiteless, syrupy black. His hair hung in grubby curls at his shoulders, long as a girl's. His trousers were snaggle-toothed in the hem and his feet still lacked boots. There was a nasty, healing wound on his face. The arbor threw striped shadows over him; his gaze lay weightily on me. He ignored my question and said, "Have you been to the forest? Everything's charcoal."

I hadn't been among the sightseers who had trekked the hills marveling at the fire's arid legacy—my parents sneered at such easily amused minds—but my father had led a party of important men on an official inspection of the burn, and he'd brought home char on his shoes. "You shouldn't do things like that," I said.

Finnigan lifted an eyebrow. "What things?"

"You know. It's wrong to burn the forest."

Finnigan smiled wolfishly. "But I'm *allowed* to do wrong things. We agreed, remember? You swore."

I set my jaw; I was still on my knees. Naturally I remembered our poisonous promise, but I hadn't expected him to take to his task so dramatically. I reminded myself he was wild and uneducated, and doubtlessly in need of a guiding hand. I said, "But the forest is your friend, isn't it?"

He pondered this, brushing his knuckles on the feathery petals of a rose, walking his fingers from thorn to thorn. Perhaps he'd never realized it before—that, being wild, other wild things were his allies. He looked across the yard. "When the forest burns, it grows back," he said. "It grows back stronger than before."

"Houses don't grow back," I answered. "Cows and sheep and horses don't grow back. All the animals that live in the forest—they don't grow back when they burn."

He glanced at me. "They would die anyway."

"When they're *supposed* to. When they're old."

His brown face flushed. "You can't tell me what to do."

"It's wrong, though—"

"It's wrong, it's wrong!" He kicked the earth, wheeled away. "Shut up, you kook! I can do what I like!"

I shrank back into the flowers and leaves. "Don't call me that. I'm not a kook. You know it's wrong to hurt things that haven't hurt you. That's not the rules."

"Oh yeah?" wailed Finnigan. "What about your brother? What had *he* done to *you*?"

My mouth snapped shut. "That's not the same. That was an accident, I told you."

Finnigan watched me for a moment; his anger dropped away. He lay down on the warm earth, quiet as a pup. "I forgot the story," he said. "Tell me again."

My bones are very close to my skin — there's no buffer of fat on me. I weigh perhaps as much as a small suitcase carrying the necessities of a night. The pillows and blankets that coddle me weigh much more than I do. Yet I lie on this mattress so heavily that I ache, I feel burdened as if by padlocks — I fear that if I fell from this bed I would crash straight through the floor. Sarah shifts and adjusts me regularly, to keep the heaviness from settling; nonetheless my flesh breaks and tears. My brother Vernon had no such careful attention during the course of his short life. The places where bone has broken the skin are the places that remind me of him.

He was born three years before me, but he was never the elder of us—how could he be, when his brain did not develop beyond the small damp cake it had been at birth? I grew up in his birdy shadow, his weak cries familiar to me from my cradle, the peculiar scent of him—his powdery skin, his soaking chin—as recognizable as the smell of smoke. He rarely left his bedroom, having scant propulsion of his own; new sights and sounds excited him, set him howling like a gibbon, a noise my mother found unbearably mortifying and not to be heard by the neighbors. So Vernon was confined, almost always, to a single room at the back of the house, and when I see him in my mind it is always with the walls of the room rising around him, the ceiling, the floor, the door. He could not walk but rather *clattered*, and an inability to hoist himself any higher than his elbows meant the view from the window was largely denied him. He had no strength or freedom.

He was whiteness, like me. His skin was snowy-white. His hair, which my mother kept cropped, was prickly like a summer lawn, wan as schoolyard chalk. He wore nothing but a nappy, which was bleached ivory from dryings in the sun. The walls and ceiling of his room were white, as was the porcelain handle on the door. His eyes were blue, as are mine. His lips were a childish pink.

He was not cheerless. As a boy I was convinced he loved me. He would rattle his cot and snort merrily when I slipped into the room. He was easily entertained with a song, a toy, a waggle of his toes. If I am thin now, he was always thinner, and when he was happy his scrawny arms would wave like the wings of a chick. He could not talk, but he could gurgle, and he was capable of joy.

He could also cry. It was the greatest blight in a blighted life. When he was not gurgling or sleeping he was crying, the bored, insufferable yowl of the tired toddler. It was his natural state of being: wet-faced and snot-nosed, ribboned with saliva, his bland face rosy with a woe he could not explain or comprehend, dribbling out a soulless sound that was, I decided, the sound of the boy-he-was grieving for the boy-he-should-have-been. The idea, I knew, was fanciful. I knew Vernon wept simply because there was nothing he could say and nothing else he could do.

It was this bleating, pathetic, constant noise that made my mother loathe him so. It was his inability to be soothed or commanded or frightened into silence. Vernon's crying was the most defiant thing my mother had ever encountered. And my mother looked with hatred upon anything that defied her.

Vernon was not a secret — everyone in Mulyan knew of his twilighted existence. To my mother's and father's faces, and mine, the townspeople sympathized. *You're good to your brother, aren't you, Anwell? It's nobody's fault, Harry; these things happen. Beth, you're a saint.* In the streets of Mulyan, outside the grocer or the auto repair, my father shrugged off such platitudes; at home he feigned obliviousness to the presence of the child. Responsibility for Vernon fell to my mother, who, on the main street, called him her *blessing* and *life's joy*. At home, he was a curse on her. The people who sympathized to her face whispered, when her back was turned, that she was rightly cursed. I never saw such falseness, such extremes of truth and lie, such coldness of the human heart as I did in those first seven years of my life, when Vernon was alive.

Let him starve to death then, Mother would rage, throwing down the plastic bowl that held his mushy food. Mush on the floor, mush on the walls, mush plastered round the child's locked mouth. He disgusts me, I feel ill. His father won't stoop to feed him. And Vernon would howl. I can do it, I would say, Mother, here, let me.

Rub his face in it, she'd sometimes say. That will teach him. Even a mongrel can be house-trained. God help me,

I wish he'd never been born; and she'd run his bath cold or too warm.

Vernon, I'd breathe, past the bars of his cot, you should die. You will be safer if you die. You might be happier. The doctor said he could live forever, there was no reason he wouldn't grow old. I loved Vernon, but I would lie awake listening to him and I'd pray for a snake to slide in his bed, hope for an illness that would finish him fast, dream that some collector of damage would take my brother away. Such wishing brought tears of shame to my eyes, but inside I must have known that Vernon was a curse on my life, too. He was mine — my concern. Away from him, I worried. I would run home from school hysterical with fear that one of my imagined tragedies had overtaken him. I would patiently spoon into his mouth his mangled evening meal. I would bathe him, soap his prickle-field head, and dry him with a towel. I'd hide my face behind the towel and play peekaboo with him, and he would scoff and gurgle. It made me feel terrible, his pleasure in that baby's game. I would count for him his fingers and toes: *Look, ten. Vernon, you're ten.* He didn't understand a word. I'd tuck him safely in his cot, then creep away to worry. I'd greet the morning worried, worry throughout the day. At seven years old I didn't know it was possible to exist in a state other than disquiet. Don't cry, Vernon; hush, hush, don't cry. You'll make your mama angry.

The last day was a Sunday, and Mother too ill to go to church. She was frequently the victim of migraines that could shatter her for days. The curtains would be drawn in her bedroom, the sheets of the big bed turned back, water brought for the cooling of her forehead, and the door inflexibly closed. I imagined her lying in dimness, motionless as an effigy, and the shape of her pain was the shape of a shut door, its color ivory.

My father, dressed for church, told me I must stay home with Vernon. Experience told me what he meant. I was to keep my brother quiet. Were his fussing to invade the sickroom, my mother's head would cave in or explode. I went to my room and shed my Sunday-best gladly—I did not enjoy church. My father departed and I was left with the door-of-pain and Vernon, who was cooing peacefully.

Another thing I understood: that Father, unusually free, would not come directly home from church, that he would find time-consuming distractions between there and here. When the gate clicked shut behind him I wandered the hall aimlessly, savoring this rare chance to reign. It must not, I knew, be wasted.

I decided to give Vernon his lunch early—food some-times made him sleepy. Once he was asleep, I would be more at liberty than I'd ever been. I could hang over the side fence and watch our neighbor Cuttle's television. There was no television in our house, but Mr. Cuttle didn't mind me peering through his window. Occasionally he was kind enough to crank the volume so I could hear. We shared a taste for cartoons.

I mashed a banana for Vernon and warmed it on the stove, adding milk and a little sugar. I carried the meal and a cloth to his bedroom, where he lay in a tangle in the cot. He grinned and snuffled to see me. I maneuvered his limbs until he was propped upright, then waved the bowl under his nose. "Look, Vernon! Banana!"

He seemed eager, smacking his lips. When I brought the spoon to his mouth, however, he jerked his head away. "Banana!" I reminded him. "You like banana."

He gazed at me with watery eyes, flapping his hands in a fret. I knew what the problem was. Vernon couldn't tell the time, he didn't even know what a clock was, but he knew it wasn't lunchtime. His life ran to a routine that never varied, and he liked it that way. Routine gave his addled existence some order, and by bringing his lunch early I was undermining the mainstay of his world. I'd known he wouldn't like it, and I'd expected him to fight. But this was a morning unlike others for me, and I was steelishly determined to make it different for Vernon, too. In his dunderheaded refusal to adapt, he was standing between myself and happiness. I hardly ever got the chance to watch cartoons. "Just *eat* it," I begged. "Banana, Vernon, look!"

I zoomed the spoon into my own mouth, ate a dollop of the creamy mess. Vernon squeezed his eyes shut, whimpered flutily. I put the spoon to his lips and he batted it blindly away. Banana splattered the rubber sheet. I felt time getting away. "Please, Vernon?"

Sometimes he could be asked nicely, and he would comply. Not this morning; he thrashed his head. I thought perhaps he wanted to be left alone. That was allowed, he could be alone. In his cot he'd come to no harm, and I could make regular rushes from the fence to his window to check that he was indeed all right. I wiped the banana off the sheet, hauled up the cot wall, and made for the door. I was almost through it when Vernon whined. I hesitated, looking back. He had his face jammed between the bars. He wanted me to stay. He would not eat or sleep or entertain himself; he'd decided I must stay. A quill of hatred spiked in me. "No. Anwell's busy, Vernon."

He stared at me with eyes like blue stones and gave a short, shrill shriek; the sparrows browsing on the lawn burst into the sky. I shut the door quickly and waved my hands to quieten him. "Anwell's busy!" I could hear the theme song of the cartoons. "Vernon, be a good boy!"

He curled his lip and I knew he didn't agree, I knew he was brewing a bloodcurdling howl that would wake my mother and ruin the day. I thought fast. Maybe I could take him outside and let him lie in the grass. I could carry him easily, although he was bigger than me. He wasn't allowed in the front garden, but the rear yard was private — only the birds would see him there. It wasn't the best solution — he'd eat the grass, get covered in dirt — but at least he would be quiet, and far from the door-of-pain. I was instantly decided: time was getting away. I lowered the wall of the cot and slid my hands under his arms. "Vernon come outside!" I enthused. "See the flowers? See the clouds?"

But he looked at me uncivilly, and twisted himself away. I grappled for him, he kicked at me, he threw himself back like a mule. His head hit a post of the cot and he yelled with outrage, his face instantly awash with tears. He wasn't crying, he wasn't hurt: he was Vernon at his worst. I clapped my hands, bounced on my toes, knotted in brittle frustration. Today Mr. Cuttle might open the window, might let me choose a chocolate from the selection he kept on a tray. "Birdies!" I sang madly. "Come see the birds, Vernon!"

I reached out again, and he lashed at me. His fingernails, kept square and short, were nonetheless sharp as kitten claws, and shaved strips of skin from my cheek. The pain of it rocked through me, chased by revulsion and hatred. My hand came up and slapped him hard across the face.

Vernon gasped—he sucked in all the air in the room. He straightened his shoulders with dignity, and filled the house with his scream. With one palm pressed to my wounded face, I could only block one ear. He arched his back and screamed again, purple and green with rage. I put my hand over his mouth and he jerked away, threshing his legs, sucking in air, screaming again.

I was only seven and they would say I wasn't thinking, but that is not true. In those moments, though I was dazed, I considered many things. I felt a plasma wetness between the fingers at my face. I knew I wasn't going to be watching any cartoons. I felt sad enough to cry over this rare day destroyed. I felt bad for hating Vernon, yet the sight of him—his tongue wobbling like a fish, his nappy working loose at the waist, bubbles erupting out of his nose — made me despise him all the more. I had lost my pity for him, I'd joined my parents on their icy plateau. And my mother would surely be woken by the commotion, and when my father came home I would be lectured and whipped.

I thought I heard mutterings from her room already.

I told them later I'd tried to comfort him, but that isn't really true. "Shh, shh," I moaned, but the great tide of noise that Vernon made drowned out these mousy sounds.

He simply roared.

His mouth was stretched as wide as it would go. His lips were jaundice-yellow. I imagined his skull shattering beneath the force of his scream. My hand groped for the cloth, and jammed it into his mouth.

Immediately the scream was muffled. His eyes flew open in surprise. From the room-of-pain along the hall, I heard sounds. My only thought now was to hide — to hide myself from my fate and to hide the monster I'd made of my brother. I needed to put him somewhere that would contain his noise and keep him safe, and hide him until this mayhem went away. He was breathing like a blown horse, his frail rib cage heaving. I wrapped my arms around his waist and dragged him from the cot. He was light and stunned, and he did not struggle. I hoisted him up and opened the door and made my way through the house, unsteady but desperate, determined. Vernon lay like a dog in my arms, his face patched rosy, his hands moving lostly in the air. The door to the laundry was open and the door of the unused refrigerator kept there was likewise off its latch. I bundled Vernon to my chest and used a knee to dislodge the refrigerator's metal racks, which clanged one after another to the floor. In their place I shoveled Vernon, who fitted the space easily. He folded onto the refrigerator floor, his hands tucked in his lap. I shut the door before he could escape. It swung, a great slab, and the rubber seal stuck tight.

I slumped against it, panting.

When I gathered myself and stepped back to look, there was no sign of him. The fridge stood silent and white as a secret. And the house was mercifully quiet. Only my ears were ringing.

It would take him some time to calm down. I went to the bathroom and climbed on a chair and looked into the mirror. Across my left cheek blazed three scarlet streaks. I put a wet cloth to them and the coolness eased the pain. The mirror showed my hair bedraggled, my eyes shining with tears. My clothes were damply mottled, from cradling

Vernon to me. My knees were trembling like jelly. I brushed my hair, washed my face, cupped my hands beneath the tap to drink. I could smell my brother and also banana. I vowed never to speak of this.

Feeling better, and now repentant, I headed back to the laundry. I would take him outside, or whatever he liked. The cartoons were probably over. Everything had gone so wrong this morning. I was glad Vernon couldn't talk.

"Anwell."

I whirled on my heels at the laundry door. My mother stood towering behind me. Her long pale hair was fanned at her elbows, she wore a nightgown that reached the floor. Its hem was baubled with dust-balls. Her gaze was distant, she was holding the wall. I thought her lips were bleeding, then saw they were merely red. "What is going on?" she asked. The words came out ponderously, one at a time.

"Nothing, Mama," I breathed.

"What was that noise? Anwell—I heard a noise."

My throat was arid, my lips cracked. "I don't think it was anything, Mama."

I stood barely as high as her angular hip, my face at the back of her hand. My terror had congealed like concrete inside me. I might have buckled, bent at the knees; instead I stood solid as a tree.

She glanced toward the flyscreened back door. "Where is your father?"

" . . . At church."

"Where is your brother?"

"In his room."

Her eyes pecked like crows along the hall. Her head craned slowly about. She stared down at me: "You liar," she said. "His room is empty. I walked past it just now."

I felt blood flooding through my body, I saw it spread on the floor. I remembered, then, how young I was, how easily trapped and deceived. A whirlwind of panic whipped up inside me. "Mama," I muttered, and couldn't think what to say. In every direction reared horror and lies. My mind raced like a rat in a wheel, my heart squeezed and convulsed and pained.

My mother reached out a quivering hand and laid it on my shoulder. The day was warm, her hand burned. She licked her lips and painstakingly said, "What have you done with him, Anwell?"

I could not help it — I was only a child. In an instant I composed a story and prepared myself to tell it. But first I did something very true of a child. My eyes left my mother's face and dashed to the refrigerator. They touched its flank and sprang away, a glance over and done in a

GABRIEL

second. But when I looked back at my mother, she was not looking at me. She was looking at the refrigerator. "Anwell," she sighed.

"Yes, Mama?"

" . . . Where is your brother?"

I could not say, I could not dredge the words. So I said, "In the garden, Mama."

There was a brief silence. "Are you sure."

I was terrified of her. Her mind was quick. Yet she'd believed me—I had outwitted her. Inside my chest, a child leaped. "Yes, Mama. He's outside. I didn't want him to wake you."

I prayed Vernon would stay quiet just a few moments more.

Mother's sights shifted suddenly, lurching back to me. She smiled thinly, and smoothed my hair. "Mama isn't well," she whispered. "She's been asleep all morning."

I nodded vigorously, and dared to say, "You should go back to bed, Mama."

Her smile lingered. "Shall I?"

I swallowed and was speechless: I had reached the end. Mother rocked vaguely, her hand still on my head. Her blue eyes looked salty, marine. "You're a good boy, Anwell," she said. She turned away slowly, as if she were

67

old, and shuffled along the hallway. Her fingers brushed the rosebud walls. She did not know it, but I scurried in her wake. I wanted to be certain that she would disappear. She walked slowly, she drifted, I almost bumped into her. But finally she reached her room and wafted through the door. It shut with a click. I pushed on it carefully, and was certain it was closed.

Then I ran down the hall, almost skipping. The torturous clouds were gone, I was giggly with glee. I burned with love and pity for Vernon. I had never felt that way.

When I opened the refrigerator door he fell out as a jumble of angles, like books spilling from a high shelf. At the same time he seemed boneless, floppy as a rag. He somersaulted on the lino and lay still. His color was blue.

I pulled the cloth from his mouth. His eyes were swollen but not shut. I bit my lip, I shook him, tapped his chest and spoke his name. I knelt on the floor beside him and didn't know what to do. Small cat-sounds of distress piped up from my throat. I leaned very close to him and willed him to move. The wetness on his face had dried and marked his cheeks with snail trails. His hands and feet were perfect, tinged faintly blue. All around him rose the sweet odor of banana.

I dared not call my mother. I sagged on the floor, paralyzed. I did not want to stay, yet I didn't dare to leave. I sensed that he was dead, but wasn't sure if death was forever. It seemed best to stay nearby, in case the chance came to make everything changed. So Vernon and I stayed where we were until my father arrived, but no chance came to change.

It was the first time I'd told the story to anyone. The telling left me drained. I'd been gouging holes into the soft earth and now my fingers were filthy. "Vernon never hurt me, not on purpose. Not one day in his life."

Finnigan had been snapping thorns from the canes and sticking them with spit to his nose: he had a dozen gray horns sprouting now, and no room for any more. He had also been plucking petals and letting them fall, and now knelt in a ring of crimson. He glanced at me with his hyena eyes. "You didn't mean to hurt him, either. That was just an accident."

I nodded. I hadn't meant it. It was a relief, to be understood.

Finnigan chewed his lip, thinking. "Maybe it was an accident that things died in the fire. Maybe I didn't mean that, either."

He glanced at me and smiled hopefully, and I smiled in return. We needed each other's forgiveness, and gave it. "Don't tell anyone," I said.

"No. Don't you tell about the fires."

"No, I won't."

Finnigan knocked the thorns from his nose and wiped it dry of spit. "Anyway," he said, "you were just a kid. You didn't know any better. Your mother—it's her fault. Your mother's and your father's. They should have been looking after him, not you."

Tiny candles of satisfaction flared in me. It is good to have a friend who thinks the same as you. I said, "If you like burning things, there's other things you could burn."

He looked at me with interest. "Like what?"

I shrugged. "Lots of people have things. One boy at school—he knocked me over with his bike. It's a new bike, it's nice. He doesn't even deserve it."

Finnigan chewed a nail, musing on this. "Some things deserve to get burned."

"Well, I don't know." I looked away. Maybe I had said too much. I didn't want to be involved. "I just think that if you're brave enough to burn the forest, you're brave enough to do lots of things."

He said nothing, looking elsewhere. He was hovering like a hawk above Mulyan, gazing down on a timber town.

Like an animal he kept his own schedule, and later when he vanished he left behind plucked petals and rose thorns. I did my best to sweep them up but my father discovered the damage, of course, and sniffed the rose scent on my palms. I took five cuts without protesting my innocence — I couldn't prove Finnigan had been in the yard. More than that, I did not care to speak his name aloud.

FINNIGAN

Surrender and me head back into town. The forest wafts off my clothes and his fur. Decay and pine, thin freezing air. Mulyan is hushed on this cold afternoon, it's a ghost-town of houses and roads. Behind the walls, though, there'll be gossip, the tin roofs will be scorching. There'll be biscuits and tea and enemies made sudden friends because they're boiling over with gossip, tripping over their tongues.

Have you heard.

I know they found.

I don't envy.

They're saying it's.

They'll say *There but for the grace of God go I*, as if murder's something that gets shared around nice and fair and square.

Mulyan is two rows of stores, one facing the other, rising over a hill that's the crippler of old biddies and the curse of their pie-eyed sons. The shops get tatty over the rise, locked up, empty, fly husks at the glass. These dead stores say, *This town won't last.* Well, nothing does.

In the lane behind the shops Surrender and me fossick. We're just a pair of stray cats, spilling rubbish, prowling round. Whatever we find I put in my shirt, for eating or inspecting later. In the hills there's many places we call home, hollow trees, wombat holes, shanties I've built using timber filched from the tray of the carpenter's truck. Our booty is brought to these hidden places that even wild animals avoid.

Maybe I give the impression we don't like company, living like this in the hills. Nothing, however, gives me greater pleasure than having a little chat. Some of Mulyan's finest citizens have met me, including Gabriel's mother and father. I don't know who they thought I was, but they didn't like my tone. I've spoken to the one that Gabriel calls Sarah, who took me in her stride. "Nice to meet you," she actually said, and held out a hand.

Not everyone's like that. Gabriel's doctor, for instance, has no sense of humor. I met him once, years ago, when the angel was hardly ill—when, if he'd wanted, he could have shrugged off this dreary long-winded expiring. "That boy's malingering," I said, being funny, but the doctor simply went puce. *Laugh*: I nearly popped. My *favorite* person is Constable McIllwraith—any chance I get, I have a word with him. "Howyoudoin Eli?" I'll say. Everyone in Mulyan likes him now, but there was once a time when they would have stoned him in the square. Back then they said he wasn't up to the job, and hexed him when his back was turned. Then, I was one of the few friends he had, but he seems to have forgotten that now.

Plenty of others have heard from me. I'm fond of leaning over a sleeper and whispering in his ear, I like snickering and whispering in the space between walls. The ones warming backsides on the hotel's hearth and the ones bent over schoolbooks and the ones raking leaves from the lawns—most of these have heard from me, although they couldn't say exactly how. I'm the voice of reason, of conscience, of spooks. For some I'm the voice that's little by little sending them mad.

None of this matters anyway, this is a waste of time. Surrender's watching with his kind copper eyes and I jump up, abandoning fun and games. Now the bones are found, the heat will turn up. The spiders will start crawling down the walls for Gabriel. It's time, I think, to visit the angel. Come, Surrender. Are you pretty, boy?

GABRIEL

They'll want to speak to me, now the bones are found. That poor simpleton McIllwraith, from whom Finnigan derives such amusement; who knows who else. They'll come on bent knees to my bedside, furrow-faced and *sotto voce*, breaking the news as if it's news to me. Already I can smell them in the room, the cloistered reek of damp suits and the mud they'll track in on their shoes. I see them jostle, knocking elbows, imperiling the jug and tray. They'll want to get close, to see the look on my face; they'll want, out of fear of the illness, to keep away. "We've identified a female," they'll say. "Do you recognize the clothes?"

Suddenly, my lungs seize: ursine claws split my ribs, bow my spine like a hook. Gruesome slugs of blood spit across the floor. I gasp for air, fight for it, my heart thuds with terror. Flame rears inside my throat, bells clang inside my ears; my legs jump epileptically, fighting off my fate. Tears race away from my eyes, my bones are dragged apart. I remember, through tortured blackness, Vernon stuffed with cloth.

Sarah comes running, though I'm too blind to see. Against my sweating face she rams the shell of an oxygen mask. The clear clean plastic is instantly spotted with blood. My body takes minutes to calm down, to slow the thud and still the bells. My mind, though, quietens in moments. In my mind I've largely accepted death — it's only my body that hasn't. It has a right to protest, I suppose: in the remote likelihood of an afterlife, it knows it isn't invited.

My nightshirt is dotted and Sarah slips it off. While she rustles in the cupboard for a replacement I look down at my chest. My flesh is the color of watery milk; veins crisscross me like circuitry. My forearms are speckled with puncture wounds, peepholes into my being. Where the spike of the drip invades my arm the skin is tender and pink. My stomach falls away emptily. My ribs are like steps, and I wonder to where.

I want all of this finished — I want them come and gone. I want the questions answered and notes taken and then I want them gone. I don't want them to be here, if and when she comes.

Unless she has already been. "Sarah," I say, "has anyone come?"

Sarah shakes her head. No.

"You'd tell me if someone had, wouldn't you?"

She wraps a hand around my own. She wouldn't lie to me.

The first time I saw Sarah, I was just a boy, and she was just an image in a black-and-white photograph. Her hair was pulled up in a ponytail, her dress was fit for a party, and on the wooden fence behind her was a curled, sleeping cat. On the flip side of the photograph a few inky words were written. *Sarah, age 12.* There was a date below the words, and I counted on my fingers: Sarah would be grown-up now, unimaginably old. *Sarah:* she had sent me toys in paper-wrapped parcels, money folded inside birthday cards. Gazing at her image, my heart was filled with warmth. I took the photograph to the kitchen and showed it to my mother. "That's Father's sister, isn't it, Mama?"

My mother plucked the photograph from my fingers. Immediately I realized my mistake. Mother dropped the image into the bin, said, "That's the best place for her."

I stared at the smug-mouthed bin. I asked, "What did she do wrong?"

Mother pushed the rolling pin with an angry, silent power. I thought she'd chosen not to hear. Unexpectedly she said, "Your dear aunt Sarah didn't want me in the family. As if they were royalty! As if I got better than I gave."

I gazed at her, struggling to understand. Something bad, something about families, something that hurt my mother's feelings. With a child's dumb loyalty, I was indignant on her behalf. Yet I could not shake the suspicion that *Sarah* meant good things to me. "She used to send me presents, didn't she? A car, and other things."

A corner of my mother's mouth twisted tight. She ceased crushing the pastry and looked down at me. "Junk," she said. "Cheap things that always broke. I told her that we did not need her charity."

I looked at the floor. A worm of pastry had fallen there — in a moment my mother would tread on it. I wanted to say that I rather liked both junk and charity. Instead I put Sarah on a shelf in my mind and shut a glass door over her. She stayed there, ponytailed, perfect: years would pass before I spoke her name again. When I became ill, I begged for her.

The drug is making me woozy. My fingers flutter under Sarah's hand. "I'm frightened," I say.

"I know."

"I'm sorry."

She smoothes hair away from my face. "Sleep now. You'll feel better."

I want to believe her; but I'm not safe. My heart is wrung by memories. My mother and father argued on the day I found the photograph. They argued in knifelike whispers, so the neighbors wouldn't hear. I, the cause of the trouble, had my possessions rummaged through. Trinkets and tidbits I'd amassed were piled into the rubbish.

I shiver under swords of fear. "I don't want my parents here. Don't let them in the room."

"I won't, Gabriel."

"They have a key—"

"I know. But I'm here. I'll keep them away. Now sleep."

"All right," I say, "I will," and she leaves. But nothing brings me peace anymore.

There was no telling what he would do, or when. I was not so bold as to think I had any influence over him, that he was in any way under my control. I felt sorry for the town, which went about its business in its usual dozy way. The people had relegated the bush fire to history. To them, the word *arsonist* signified someone who, having loosed his havoc on our hills, had taken his reptilian pleasures elsewhere.

And Finnigan was not one to rush himself. Maybe half a year passed without incident — certainly winter did. I read and reread the worn word on the fence, swept away leaves that fell on it, dried raindrops with my sleeve. I was twelve, and I knew now that Finnigan was not a tiger in the dark. He was real, and he was hibernating somewhere. Yet when Jeremie Tool's outhouse caught fire, I didn't automatically blame him; there had been lightning above the town that night, and this seemed the likely culprit. It wasn't until I found, on my windowsill, a small, dented, flame-blacked doorknob that my blood went cool. I remembered running a stick along Tool's wooden fence, inciting his dogs into strangled rage. Tool had burst from the house, shrieking at me; I had scuttled home scarlet-faced. I had told Finnigan. Now something had burned. I buried the scalded doorknob as deep as I could go.

Everything happened just as I imagined.

Soon after Tool's outhouse went up in smoke, the clothes on Bushell's clothesline were reduced to charred tatters. Jammy Bushell, the youngest son, was a bully and a pincher, and insufferably vain.

Mrs. Henry Nightingale woke to see her azalea hedge in flames.

The front fence of the Wells house could be seen for miles when it burned, and the grimy stink of kerosene palled the town for days. Limerick Wells was a boy of no significance but he had nominated me for the role of princess in the annual school play.

It was only after this that Constable Eli McIllwraith, our newly appointed law enforcer who was, in the minds of his elders, insultingly raw and underaged, conceded that Mulyan was being stalked by an arsonist. The evidence seemed to point to a resident of the town or its surrounds. We were told to be on the lookout for anything suspicious; property owners were advised to leave their dogs unchained. Finnigan smiled at this: he liked dogs.

Those early blazes were to prove a gentle introduction to his work. Finnigan did not grow out of, but rather into, his pastime. Committed to his undertaking, well fitted to the work, he would create for Mulyan a legend, for the burnings would continue sporadically year after year. Months would go by unsmoked, but people soon realized that was a lull. The firefly was victim to an unquenchable itch. Night would quilt the valley, the world would be at peace — then the bell would jangle at the town hall, the siren would whir into life, the roosters, confused, would crow at the moon, and flames would be leaping like jaguars for the stars.

The barn that had stood for ninety years on the hill behind Torquil's farm, the subject of innumerable watercolors and the site of many a fumbled first kiss.

The clubroom on the edge of the sporting oval, together with the scoreboard on which generations of bored time-keepers had scratched their beloved's name.

The racecourse stables, which were already falling down.

Raffe Lowe's notorious car, for the purchase price of which he'd sacrificed three fingers laboring at the lumberyard.

The clubroom that was built to replace the original one, which had burned.

The citizens of Mulyan could hardly contain their out-rage. None but small-minded adolescents found amuse-ment in the arsonist's escapades. A string of names was cast up as suspects, their owners interrogated by McIllwraith. Soon it became evident that unscrupulous souls were volunteering as suspects the names of those who'd done them wrong. Anger flourished, and division. It was around this time that Finnigan began to shadow McIllwraith, and

learned much by studying the Constable's habits and tech-
nique. The smudged hyena was cultivating a mind as sleek
and slippery as an eel.

One balmy afternoon in spring I sat with the criminal
on the shoulder of Cotton's Pinch, looking down on farms
small enough to sit in a palm, on cattle the size of square
sluggish ants. I asked. "Are you ever going to stop?"

Finnigan's hair was long, ragged as a yard-dog's scruff.
He lay on the rocky earth, picking his teeth with a twig.
At thirteen he slept in creek beds and trees; he never
spoke of his parents or of the place in the mountains
where he'd been raised. His eyes were jet and unnerving.
It pleased me to think that he was a member of an un-
discovered species, half-human half-beast half-storybook-
goblin, which roamed the world wildly, wreaking chaos.
He replied, "When there's none left who deserve it."

"But what had Raffe Lowe done? He loved that car."

Finnigan sneered. "That car stunk. He drove too fast.
Anyway, a car is a stupid thing to love."

"What about the flower shop?"

Earlier that week a burning bottle of petrol had shattered
the window of the produce store run by the Gilligan twins.
Minnie and Rose sold homemade jam, sickly sweets, useless objects, cloth and lace, and flowers which, once taken

home, tended to rapidly wilt. The shop was ancient, and tinder-dry. The fire had skyrocketed sparks into the night; they sailed down gently to lie all around the twins, who sat howling on the road. The light of the flames stained the sisters orange, and reddened their long pallid faces. The fire, the dark, the howling, the twins—somebody thought the only thing missing was a cauldron, and that somebody was me.

I hadn't, till then, known the depth of my grudge.

One day when I was six or seven I had stood beside a bucket of jonquils as Minnie, the older twin, suggested with a smile that I was concealing a candy horse in my pocket, having plucked it from a jar on the counter while Minnie's mind was elsewhere, measuring curtain material. "You'll have to watch that one, Beth," she said. "He's a crafty fellow."

Perhaps she'd meant my mother to take this as a compliment. Mother chose to take it another way. "How dare you!" she shrilled. "How dare you! You think I'd raise a thief? Anwell, turn out your pockets! This woman wants to see what you have in them."

Standing on the floury floor, my blood dried up, my head an empty cup, there was nothing for it but to abandon my frame to its fate. When a certain degree of horror is reached, one must go—one can't stay. My hands fished in my coat pockets and drew out not one but two algae-green horses prancing on lollipop sticks.

My mother made a choking sound, as if she'd swallowed her tongue.

Minnie was trying uselessly to make amends. "He's a boy!" she cried. "Boys are like that, all of them! If I had a penny for every sweetie that's gone into the pocket of a boy!"

My mother was taking no notice of the shopkeeper: her eyes were like pickaxes buried in me. "Put those things on the counter," she hissed. "Go outside and wait for me."

"Let him keep them, Beth. The loss won't break us—"

I stepped around Mother to lay the horses on the counter. They cavorted greenly, one behind the other. The first had been for me, the second one for Vernon. He wouldn't have eaten his, of course, but that didn't mean I shouldn't offer. I turned, and stumblingly crossed the floor. As the door wheezed shut behind me I heard, "You can keep your material. It's revolting, anyway."

At home, too disgusting to be seen, I was sent to stand in a corner of the yard and stayed there until night fell, and for long after that. I was brought inside at midnight, drowsy and gray with cold.

Finnigan was watching a flock of pigeons looping the town. He said nothing—he never spoke unless he had to.

My mother soon returned to being a customer of the twins, the equivalent stores in neighboring towns having higher prices and less decency, but I could never again bring myself to push past the wheezing door. I wouldn't see inside the flower shop again until the fire burned the frontage away.

I lay down beside my friend and looked up at the clouds. Finnigan nodded at the swooping birds, said, "Pigeons make good pie."

I smiled. The air felt warm and fresh in me. I thought about what he'd told me, and everything that had burned. I said, "So you're only punishing people who deserve it."

Finnigan stayed silent, nibbling a twig.

"That's not really a *bad* thing to do, is it? I mean, that's what *God* does, isn't it?"

Finnigan glanced at me and splintered the twig and I could feel his mind ticking. I could feel him understanding what I said, and not liking it. Instinct warned me to be quiet, but I continued gamely on. As a partner in the pact, I wouldn't be censored by fear of him. I said, "Anyone would think *you* were the angel, not me."

His hand flashed out, lashing at me; he scrambled to his feet. "Don't you call me names!" he cried. "Don't you ask me questions!" And in an instant he'd disappeared down the steep flank of Cotton's Pinch, leaving me behind with a stinging wound and a sense of satisfaction. My point, I felt, had been made. I didn't want to be associated with any devil whose doings were clouded by morality. There was no point to our pact — no point to my goodness, no point to *him* — unless his wickedness was a whole-hearted, ungovernable thing. To make things right and proper, both of us had to be pure.

He had run off in a rage: when, in the months that followed, a crop was torched and the belltower destroyed and the antique sign that welcomed tourists was reduced to a pile of cinders I understood this was Finnigan's sullen, wantonly violent, message to me. Crusader Watts spent weeks crafting a new sign, only to see it, too, turned to charcoal: *See?* said Finnigan. *See?* All across Mulyan, chaos ruled. Roderick Bunkle, the town's famed equestrian, returned from a gallop to find the stable in flames, his prized horses running berserkly over the hills. Papa and Mama Marcuzzi and their seven mousy kits watched with pleasure as their garage burned, proud to be included in the town's misery. Ms. Evelyn Pree, the school principal, lost an entire season's homebrew when her bungalow was set alight, and for three days afterward Mulyan reeked of petrol, sugar, and beer.

There was, naturally, wholesale hysteria. Mulyan had never found itself blessed with so much to seethe about. A frightened, resentful fury slicked the town like dirty grease. People woke at night plagued by hideous imaginings; they became irrational, short-tempered, and quick to take offense. They became ludicrously protective of the few worthwhile things they owned. And they hated the arsonist for making them into the creatures they'd become. At the bar of the Clover and Willow elaborate punishments were devised and made ready to receive the squirming figure of the snared culprit. In the window of the liquor shop an effigy was placed, a matchbox sitting in its hand and brain-fluff leaking from its head. "Know what we should do to him?" asked Danny Collop of Lissie Skene, the pair of them standing in the shade of the incinerated town hall. "We should hang him like in the good old days, and then we should draw and quarter him."

"What do you mean?" asked Lissie. "Draw a picture of him, you mean?"

"No, no — gut him, like he was a pig."

"Oh," said Lissie, and nodded; I took my timely leave.

Inside my own small family, it was my father who took the burnings hard. A man of solitude within his own four walls, preferring the privacy of his study and the company of his plants, he cultivated an outgoing and forthright persona when in public. He was Mulyan's only lawyer, and saw himself as the town's representative of all that was correct: as such, he took the rampage of the firebug as an attack upon himself. He would make haste to the site of each new burn, and pick through the rubble for evidence — which brought him to the attention of Constable McIllwraith, who had the gall to warn him off and thereby gained for himself a dire enemy. Helpless and frustrated, my father thrashed like a mud-mired bull. He combed great books to discover how arsonists had been cornered and dealt with in the past. His dread was that our criminal, once caught, would escape on a technicality — madness, perhaps — or would prove too young to be blasted by the full force of Justice's wrath. He voiced this concern everywhere, railing against the cunning of the crazed and underaged. In the meantime, while the felon was nameless and faceless and free, it was necessary that *someone* should shoulder the blame. Lacking a criminal, my father turned on the one charged with solving crime.

Constable Eli McIllwraith had not been born in Mulyan—had, indeed, been born in the city, which made him unacceptably alien. He was also young and inexperienced, his uniform still creased, and thus he provided good sport for the rowdy elements of town. His posting in Mulyan loosely coincided with the beginning of the firefly's reign, and when someone put these facts together a rumor went round that the policeman himself was lighting the flames. My father dismissed this idea as idiotic, a symptom of our desperation; nonetheless he had McIllwraith in his sights. Father despised incompetence, and the Constable, with his ongoing failure to apprehend the culprit, was clearly unfit for his task. So Father began planting little bombs of discontent—a mutter here, a chuckle there, an overheard sniff of derision—which soon scratched like sandpaper against Mulyan's confidence in the young man. Everyone respected my father's opinion—he was a lawyer, which meant he knew things. It wasn't wise to challenge him intellectually. But more than this, Father was simply a frightening man: devoid of humor, razored of tongue, he considered none his equal, including his wife and sons. He thought me a wood-headed cretin; Vernon infinitely repulsed him. When Father spoke, what he said was law, and it was easiest to agree.

The bombs my father scattered made life awkward for McIllwraith. Deathly silence fell when he walked into a room; murmured words and chortling proliferated in his wake. Men bragged of patrolling their land with shotguns, daring the law to interfere. Someone started a petition asking that Mulyan be sent another, more experienced policeman to sort out the mess. And soon everywhere that McIllwraith went he was watched by doubting, ridiculing eyes; every time he stepped out of his house he felt the ground shake under him.

Finnigan was not unaffected by the bitterness engulfing the town. He followed each development with interest. And when the chance came to put a spark to the powder keg that was Mulyan, he did not hesitate. Like a cat he stepped past the dozing guard and torched the town's library. No one except the guard was surprised—the surprise lay only in the fact that the building had gone uncooked for so long. But book burning is a volatile thing: I knew Finnigan had been saving the library, as a child leaves until last the choicest item on its plate. He'd kept the library in reserve until only a final straw was needed to break the camel's back in two.

Break it did, although not in equal halves: the greater part of Mulyan's incensed population sided with my father, who now openly declared the Constable incompetent and rallied the people to take the law into their hands. Some of these people had long disliked my father, his bullish manner, his uppity ways; their offspring were my school-yard torturers, callers-of-names and tippers-of-chairs. But now we shared a common foe, and our differences were laid aside. At school I enjoyed a sudden immunity, which I savored while it could last. Our policeman was spurned and sneered upon in the street; he was mocked by little children. *The sooner he goes, the better.* A city newspaper ran an article detailing our slide toward mob rule, to the indignation of all except Finnigan, who cackled delightedly. My father, meanwhile, began organiz-ing parties of men to patrol the streets. Posting guards at likely burn sites was clearly ineffective; there was, to my father's mind, a need — indeed, a *want* — to see the streets roamed by gangs. The more temperate folk of Mulyan were aghast at this turn of events; McIllwraith warned that it was only a matter of time before some innocent had his head stove in with a cricket bat. From the pulpit the priest reminded his flock that nothing is worth the price of a life, no crime unforgivable by God. My father replied that by wading uninvited into the argument, the Church was bringing itself dangerously to the attention of the godless firebug. McIllwraith answered that, with vigilantes on the prowl, he had no choice but to advise everyone to stay indoors at night. Mulyan, he said, was effectively under a self-imposed curfew. The word rocked the reason of the opposing camps: old ladies were frightened to walk to the store; young bucks bolted searchlights to the roofs of their cars and spent the night cruising the streets.

The town was never uglier. It held its breath and rocked perilously on the knife's edge.

Finnigan, by now, had been stalking McIllwraith for months, and knew him like an old friend; I, however, had little to do with the policeman, who, aware whose son I was, never tried to make a friend out of me. Perhaps he understood the grief it could cause, were I caught fraternizing with the enemy. But when Father became the leader of a gang of vigilantes, things, not unpredictably, changed. McIllwraith now had something to say, and reason to say it. I was sitting on the swings in the park with Finnigan when the outlaw nodded toward the road and said, "Look."

I looked and saw the Constable striding across the grass. It was Saturday, cold, and the park was deserted but for the three of us. I sucked in my breath, whispered, "Let's go."

"No." Finnigan idled on his swing, his toes scraped the ground. "He'll wonder why."

McIllwraith slowed as he reached us, and finally stopped. His shoes were shiny, glossed with rain. Fog unraveled from his mouth. I clutched the heavy chains of my swing, my fingers pink and white; Finnigan sat calmly. "Cold day," said McIllwraith.

"It's winter," answered Finnigan.

McIllwraith looked away; my heart jumped at my ribs. Above our heads a crying crow was blown like black rubbish through the sky. My face burned, chilled by the wind. McIllwraith was looking at me.

"You're Harry's son, aren't you? Anwell?"

He wanted to talk about Father, not the fires. It was a relief; I nodded. Finnigan spun on his swing, smiling. McIllwraith, his hands in his pockets, hugged his coat to him. "Has Harry still got men roaming round town every night?"

"Yes." The policeman surely knew it. Finnigan and I were both fourteen now, and the Constable must once have been fourteen too, yet he was wary of us, guarded. He feared, I think, that we were untrustworthy. He worried he might say something that could be used against him.

He was afraid of being seen with us; he was afraid of my father. I understood how he felt.

"What about it?" Finnigan asked. His voice jarred the silence. McIllwraith looked at him.

"It's dangerous. They're terrorizing people, not protecting them. Someone is going to get hurt."

"He wants to stop the firebug."

McIllwraith shook his head. "It's not his job. No one asked for his help. Why is he doing this?"

Finnigan shrugged, and they both looked at me. "I don't know," I said.

"He's crazy?" Finnigan offered.

"He likes everything to be under his control." I frowned, and held the statement up to the light. I'd never framed my life in so few words. *My father likes everything to be under his control.*

"Including you?" asked McIllwraith.

"Yes," I answered: including me.

"I don't want to get you into trouble. Should I walk away?"

Finnigan looked at me; I shook my head slowly. "No," I said. "This should stop."

A cloud sighed widely out of the policeman. My

hands fell from the chains to my lap. "Tell him," murmured Finnigan.

"Tell him what?"

"What?" echoed McIllwraith.

"Everything. What they're getting up to on their little midnight jaunts. Where they go, what they do — you could spoil everything for them."

I was shocked. "You *want* me to tell?"

"Would you?" McIllwraith's gaze jumped over me. "Could you?"

I faltered, uncertain. "I don't know. If he found out I was doing that . . ."

"Then don't." McIllwraith set his jaw. "If you think he'll find out, don't do it."

"But what about the fires?" asked Finnigan plaintively. "They need stopping too."

I nodded to this. "The fires have to be stopped."

"They will be stopped," said the Constable. "But not by vigilantes. Not by spreading fear through the town. That won't stop the arsonist."

"I agree," said the firebug. "That won't work."

"What your father is doing is wrong, Anwell—he's just as wrong as the arsonist is."

"He's *more* wrong," said Finnigan.

"His actions are equally dangerous—you know that yourself, don't you?"

"You don't have to persuade us," said Finnigan. "We'll do it. Why shouldn't we? The bastard deserves it."

"It will keep everyone safe," I said. "That's why I'll do it."

McIllwraith paused, the wind rifling his coat. I could not tell if he was pleased. After some moments he said, "You too, though. Remember: you need to keep safe."

Finnigan replied immediately, "And you."

"Yes," I said quietly, "you too."

The policeman blinked, and gave a slack nod. "Maybe I'll see you around," he said; then he turned and walked away. I leaned against the knotted chain and did not look at Finnigan. When the Constable had gone far enough to be small I said, "I don't think he knows it's you. He would have said something if he'd known."

"He doesn't know." Finnigan's voice was certain. "Anyway, he's not thinking about the firebug. He hates your father more. . . . McIllwraith is just a man. He has hate and vengeance. We can use that."

I rocked back and forth, scuffing the ground. The prospect of secretly undermining my father tingled my nerves, made me smug. But if I was to be caught passing information to the police, the consequences would be dire. The runty offspring of uppity parents, brother to a half-wit, the shutter and locker of refrigerator doors — I did not need branding as a traitor as well. It wanted just the smallest error to push me over the hellish edge-of-no-return. I glanced resentfully at Finnigan, who was forcing me to the brink. I felt invaded by him, fatally entwined, yet it was always me — never him — who teetered on the edge: "No more fires," I said. "Stop this now, Finnigan."

"Soon. There's things we still have to do. We can't make McIllwraith tame without fire. Without fire, there's nothing to say. You don't want to disappoint him, do you? You told him you'd help: you promised. The vigilantes are your fault, after all. All of this is your fault."

"*My* fault! Why?"

"You lit the fires as much as I did. You told me, *go out and burn.* Besides, we're reflections, blood brothers, remember? What I do, you do."

The cold wind had brought water to my eyes; I smeared them dry on my sleeve. I could smell, on the breeze, the earthen scent of him. "You remember that, don't you, Anwell?"

Something dangerous wafted from him — something not to be denied. "Yes, I remember."

He swayed on his swing. "There's one other thing."

"What?"

"It's time to make your father sorry."

I glanced up fearfully. "You'll only make him angrier. What good will that do me?"

Finnigan shrugged. "None, probably."

He stepped from his swing and walked away, casual as a cat crossing a lawn, leaving in his wake a swathe of shattered raindrops. I watched him until he disappeared in the trees. Watching him, I felt my blood shimmer. In minutes, on a cold afternoon, he had changed my life again. What he did, I must do.

And surely it worked the same in reverse.

I had not thought of that before.

Reflections, blood brothers, twins: therefore:

What I did, he must do.

My father organized his vigilantes in the disused back room of our house. He'd pinned a map of Mulyan to the wall and marked crosses at the burn sites. The men arrived after dinner each evening and stood around very seriously. The room was small and they were big men, so the air was soon made stale. It being assumed I shared my father's stance on this and every matter, my presence was permitted in the room while they talked. I made my-self useful, opening bottles, emptying ashtrays. I nodded and laughed whenever they did, knit my brow, curled my lip: I was the essence of loyalty. I stayed in the room after the men had embarked on their nocturnal cru-sade, sweeping cigarette ash from the floor, collecting the empty glasses. And Finnigan would creep near, near, sounding no more threatening than a possum or a fox, and halt in the darkness, unseen, all ears. I would open the window and hushly explain where the hunters were lying in wait. Most often it was Finnigan who relayed this news to McIllwraith, trotting down the road to the sta-tion, loitering in the shadows. Sometimes, however, his presence was required elsewhere, and it was I who ran through the fog-threaded night, I who knocked on the station-house door before ducking into the dark. "Quotation Creek," I'd whisper, when the door opened and let out the light. Once "Peyton's Lookout," once "Oxford Road." McIllwraith would nod, glance in the direction of the lookout or road. "Thank you, Anwell," is all he'd say, be-fore solemnly shutting the door. I would race home then, my heart ripping.

To begin with, I was afraid. I was afraid of getting caught, afraid my treachery glowed like a corona around me. Then, when I did not get caught, I grew to love the fear. It sang in me like wires. I'd say, at the window, to Finnigan, "I'll go." I'd fly, my blood speeding. My alliances were like friendships with lions, imperiling, incredible, the foundation of power. *Thank you, Anwell.*

Finnigan had his own use for what he heard at the window. He used the information to map his black travels through the night. Sometimes he put distance between the vigilantes and himself; other nights he followed them as a jackal follows a herd. He would light trails of tiny blazes to guide them where he wished them to go. He occasionally let them near enough to feel the breeze of his slipping away. In the torch-light they would find matches still warm from being struck. He smelled of nothing manmade, of forest and chilled air, and the tracker dogs could not distinguish him from a sapling or a rock. And my father, seeing that his quarry was quicksilver, began to fidget, forgot his flowers, became slapdash with his work. His ongoing failure to snare the arsonist ate at the town's respect for him. Mulyan had lost its serenity, been riven into factions, turned puerile with suspicion; the streets themselves were now deadly places to be seen after dark—yet still the firebug roamed free. Months wore on, the vigilantes grew bored, the town grew ashamed of how low it had sunk, and there was clearly one person to blame. My father, his glory days sliding away, was twitchy, martyred, sulky, betrayed. One night the howl of the fire bell—the sound of defeat, to Father's ears—actually made him choke. He doubled over, gagging, swept his plate to the floor. My mother's nerves were shattered; she fled to her room.

In these dying days of the burnings, I was at liberty. "He's forgotten who I am," I told Finnigan. "All he thinks about is you."

The fugitive yawned, his face to the sun. "Tell him," he said, "there's worse to come."

It was no surprise then, when, two nights afterward, my father's car exploded in flame.

The ramshackle remnants of the vigilante gang were patrolling a bridge in a fog-filled gully where, that morning, a dented petrol tin had been found. McIllwraith was ghosting them, having had Finnigan knock at the door. Father, however, had stayed home—the night was frosty, and he minded his health. The Wolseley stood, in my father's affections, on equal footing with his most prized roses. When fire bloomed inside the car, unfurling magician cloths of flame, which scorched the house and lit up the garden with orange and yellow and green, it is fair to say that Father would struggle to believe his eyes.

Hearing commotion I ran from my room and found my parents tilting like totems on the veranda, my mother clutched to my father's chest, my father pushing her away. The Wolseley was parked in the driveway and its blue bulk was swollen with molten flames, which brightened my father's pale face. I stopped on the lawn, shielding my eyes, and as the fire banked and swept I glimpsed the warped seat, the dashboard consumed, the bonnet buckled into a scream. The air was dense with toxic stink, and blankets of black smoke surfed up to the sky. Sparks arched across the lawn and fell glowing into the grass. As neighbors rushed from along the street and the hose was whipped from its prim spinning wheel, the heat of the fire forced me back until my shoulders touched the garage wall. I felt the heat slide under my clothes, felt it evaporate the water in my eyes. My hands came unbidden up to my face, and held themselves over my ears. I could not look away from the car, this planet imploding, this living thing killed, this end of some unknown world. There were a hundred people suddenly in our yard; through muffled ears I heard my father shriek as rosebushes were crushed in the press. An alarm bell was ringing and there was raucous shouting, bodies stumbling and vanishing in the dark. The windows of the Wolseley succumbed with a dull crumple. The tap was spun hard and the hose reared, gushing a torrent from its nose: water pummeled the footpath and then the garage, sprayed savagely across my face. The hose was wrestled earthward, the nose pointed at the car, and water speared into the fire's black heart; sparks raced skyward like demons. The fire hissed, dodging the spray; flames wrapped furiously around the tires and heaved out greasy smoke. The water pummeled from the hose, a torrent like a pickax or a solid blade of steel, yet nothing changed, the car still burned, the fire mobbing as bees mob a man, unrelenting, overwhelming. The hubcaps blew off one after another and clattered across the concrete. The kingly stench of petrol made the air poisonous to breathe. I stood back speechless against the wall, my hands on my ears, my face burning red, and all I could think was that Finnigan was right. *It is wondrous.*

The fire was quenched suddenly, as if the water had succeeded in puncturing a vital piece of its fiery being. It retreated, simmering, into the dark, taking with it its heat and color, its spectacular noise. In place of the grandeur stood the dripping shell of the car, the ugly, undevourable bone. Its ruined wheels sat in pools of dark liquid; it waved flags of limp white smoke. The lawn was crushed, the rosebushes bedraggled. I moved my hands from my ears to my face, and felt the heat driven into my skin.

Our neighbors were jovial; they had achieved something; they invited themselves into the house. They knew that, in this moment of goodwill, my parents wouldn't dare turn them away. I lingered outside, watching the sky clear. Charred leaves dropped from the overhanging ash. I plucked strands of singed hair from my eyes. The Wolseley continued to drip. I scoured the darkness for Finnigan, but couldn't find him

In the loungeroom my parents were being plied with whisky. Neighbors were milling around. Few of them had ever breached the privacy of the house, and they meant to remember what they saw. They searched the room for photographs and heirlooms, for anything that told tales. They scanned for sign of Vernon, our little tragedy. They took mental guesses at the value of everything on the sideboard. I supposed we disappointed them — there were no photo frames, no silver or crystal, no shrines to the lost child. My mother and father were not the type to unnecessarily decorate their lives. I hung about on the edge of the crowd, leaned against the door. Father stood in the center of the room, freakishly chipper. He clapped men on their shoulders and heartily shook their hands. "It had to happen sooner or later!" he bellowed. "I was starting to feel ignored!"

Later that night, when everyone had gone home, I heard him reminding my mother that he'd been starting to feel ignored.

The cold light of day chilled the effervescence from my father. There stood the Wolseley, destroyed. The prize-winning roses along the front fence were cooked, the lawn was a puddly quagmire. The weatherboard flanks of the house were scorched, licked by a dragon's sooty tongue. My father, having inspected the wreckage, marched down the road to the police station. Thunder rolled and lightning clashed in his furious wake. Finnigan saw him coming and dropped from a tree, skipped ahead to take up position under the stationhouse floor. McIllwraith was reading the newspaper at the counter when my father barged through the door. He listened in silence while Father shot questions as if from a gun. Where had the Constable been when the Wolseley was splashed in petrol last night? When Tool's outhouse burned, when Nightingale's hedge flared, when Bunkle's horses galloped off, when Torquil's barn collapsed to the ground; when the flower shop, the library, Lowe's vehicle, the town hall, when all of these had come to grief, where had the Constable been? The fires had blighted Mulyan for three years yet the Constable, miraculously, had never found himself where he was needed: at the right place, at the right time.

McIllwraith considered this question. "Are you saying I had something to do with the fires, Harry?"

"Don't be ridiculous!" My father laughed loudly. "Anyone could see you haven't the brains to light a camp-fire! I'm saying you're incompetent: nothing more, nothing less. I'm saying that the next time something burns in this town, you'll find yourself sweeping the streets."

Finnigan could mimic Father's voice well. He paused in the story and chuckled. We were sitting together in the chicken coop at home, and a white hen was eyeing us uneasily. "He'll do it, too," I said. "He always does what he says. He'll get McIllwraith thrown out of his job."

Finnigan was driving a needle of straw into the bed of his thumbnail. He twisted the straw counterclockwise and winced, not looking at me.

"We can't let that happen, Fin."

He slid a sheltered glance at me, as if I wearied and annoyed him. I shifted my seat on an upturned fruit box. My life revolved around the twin secrets I kept: Finnigan and McIllwraith. When I was alone, or tormented at school, the two secrets gave me pride. I did not want to lose one of them. "He trusts us. He's useful. You said it yourself."

Finnigan's attention was on his thumb. A petal of blood lay under his nail. The hen kept her eyes on us. "You have to stop burning," I said. "You must."

Still he said nothing. I could feel him contemplating throwing McIllwraith to the wolves. "Don't," I breathed. "Don't."

He snarled suddenly, flung the straw away. "Who cares?" he snapped. "I don't care."

I glanced aside, loath to anger him. Through the wired window I saw parrots grazing on the lawn. The hen hiccuped, studying Finnigan's thumb. "So you'll stop?" I dared to say.

"Who cares?" he repeated. "It doesn't matter. There's nothing left to burn."

He kept his word, as he always would; after the Wolseley, there were no more fires. Weeks, then months, went by unburned; the last vigilantes wandered home. All of Mulyan understood that the end of the attacks was not due to some victory on our part. The arsonist was simply gone: he'd died or moved on or grown bored. The gangland days of the burnings looked, in peacetime, like an unspeakable nightmare. Mulyan was critically wounded, soaked in accusations and shame. Ancient friendships had been destroyed. The town was no longer the same. And everyone looked for a place to lay the blame for all that had been and was gone.

In the past my father had been disliked; now he was purely resented. The women pressed their lips and turned away from my mother in the street. And their children, who were my schoolfellows, brought the guilt and grief and ruined friendships to school, and visited them upon me.

Life, it seemed, had returned to normal.

Except for one thing.

Days after his beloved Wolseley was destroyed, my father, still addled by the attack, did something starkly uncharacteristic of his granitelike character. He allowed himself to be talked into the adopting of a dog.

FINNIGAN

Surrender has always been mine. Before he was born, when his dam was a pup, when his sire ran youthful on streets and on hills, Surrender was already mine. I was whelped and raised owning him; laying eyes on him was like meeting an old old friend. He was a yearling then, a circus of limbs, his coat the color of clay. His tail hooked up to the sky, his eyes showed a half-moon of pink. He came already named, in honor of me: *surrender*. The angel thought *he* stopped the fires; he didn't. It was only Surrender.

Anyway, that's enough. It's not my job to look back: I go forward.

It's late afternoon. I'm on my way to see Gabriel. But first I take a detour.

I'd thought I'd find McIllwraith mooching around the bones but he wasn't, and now I'm searching. With cold evening coming to bulkily snow on the ranges and ice-muzzle the cows, the policeman's probably holed up at home. I slip like air through Mulyan's streets, which are already dim. From the houses that line the dirt road float strangulated smoke signals. My feathery friend, calling out to me. People are behind the walls, curled around news of the bones. Not since the burnings has Mulyan seen such excitement, and probably it won't ever again.

Constable Eli McIllwraith is still a young man, although not so young as he was. Country living has taken its toll on him. When he first arrived in town he was fresh and fuzzy as a peach, as pretty and innocent as Rapunzel. They sent him here, out of harm's way, because there's a widespread belief that nothing of interest ever happens in the country.

That is wrong.

In Gabriel's father, during the years of the fires, McIllwraith made for himself a vile enemy. No one gives Surrender credit for dousing the fires, but some people gave it to McIllwraith. He was the law, after all, and the firebug was now obeying it. In the eyes of some people, McIllwraith's reputation was raised. But never in the eyes of Gabriel's father, and never in the eyes of McIllwraith, either. Both of them knew that it wasn't the policeman who'd snuffed out those flames.

People have come to the bones like vultures do. They've brought cameras and notepads and questions, questions. There is a lady sitting in McIllwraith's loungeroom, a notebook lying on her lap. McIllwraith sits opposite her, crossing and recrossing his legs. Surrender and I watch all this from a hole we've dug into the ceiling.

You must feel vindicated, now the grave's found.

I'm happy things can move on, yes.

The lady writes that down.

How well did you know the boy?

Anwell. Not particularly well.

So what caught your attention about him, that day?

Various things. My instincts.

She smiles, writes that. He's not being much help.

What about you, Constable? A country town can't be too challenging for a young policeman. Will you move on too?

He shuffles. He hopes so, but doesn't say. The lady seems to guess. She lowers her pen.

I'm sure they'll realize they can make better use of you. They won't leave you here to rot. Not now.

McIllwraith shuffles, shrugs, coyly smiles. He hopes like hell so.

Mulyan. The lady thinks. Isn't this the place that was terrorized by a firebug, a few years ago?

She has lifted her pen.

We had a few incidents. We weren't terrorized.

Remind me how that panned out? The arsonist was caught, I assume?

No. We never identified him. The fires just stopped.

She is surprised. Just stopped? Know why?

I suppose he realized that sooner or later he was going to get caught.

The lady flips the cover of her notebook. Thank you for your time, Constable McIllwraith.

He sees her to the door. On the threshold she pauses, looking out to the hills. She turns and gives him a pursed-lip smile. I hope they let you out of this place. I'll cross my fingers for you.

He watches her walk away down the path; he closes and leans on the door.

I cast a glance around the roof space. From a cracked ceiling beam I break off a wooden spike. McIllwraith doesn't hear the sound of timber splintering. He crosses the room and stokes up a fire, disappears from my view while he adjusts the TV. I hear him peel off his shoes and when I see him again he is shoeless, on the couch, lying down.

The cheerful sound of cartoons rises to the sky.

GABRIEL

Evening always finds me at my illest, most ill: Sarah writes on my chart that I'm *fretful*. And why shouldn't I be? It is not nice to die.

It's getting dark: I must hurry. My illness and I are running a race to the end, and it is the swifter of us.

My father was ignorant of dog flesh: he never saw that, in Surrender, he was being sold a pup. The dog was charged with guarding the house and yard but it soon became apparent that Surrender stood aloof from material concerns. His thoughts, by and large, lay with himself. He did have guarding instincts—he guarded his privacy. He minded his own business and expected others to do likewise. When they did not—when a delivery boy woke him, when a passerby laughed aloud, when a pat on the head rubbed him the wrong way, when insultingly encouraged to fetch a ball—the perpetrator would find themselves fixed with a cold copper stare. If this warning went ignorantly ignored, Surrender would not hesitate to bite. Between my mother and father he became known as Useless Animal, but I admired his determination not to be told. He feared nothing, was the slave of no one. Another owner might have shown him the business end of a gun, but Surrender's life was saved by my parents' inability to admit to mistakes. It was vital that they appear perfect — though their first son was blighted, their second son mulish, though they'd managed to alienate themselves from everybody they knew; though their lives had foundered in a crumbling country town and though their twenty years of weddedness were years as airless as lead — because only perfection would allow them to condemn everything else as faulty. Surrender stayed, despite his contrariness, because getting rid of him — or of Vernon, or of me, or of their wedding vows — would be a public admission of error, and that would be unendurable. Finnigan smiled when I put this to him, wrinkling his nose at the sky. "They were made for each other," he said. "It would be cruel to separate them."

We were both fifteen years old that spring, although Finnigan seemed without age, the way a cat appears for much of its life, its face unchanged by time. He dressed in clothes thefted from clotheslines, from bags left outside the charity shop. He rarely spoke about anything except the future — never about where he'd come from, who or what he'd left behind. He was a beg borrow and stealer, the owner of nearly nothing. He'd loved Surrender from the moment he saw him, and the hound was likewise fonder of Finnigan than he was of anyone else. I knew that while I was at school, Finnigan and the dog accompanied each other on long patrols of the countryside; I knew, too, that they traveled at night, borrowing trucks left parked in laneways, borrowing bicycles from garden sheds, plucking fruit from laden trees, plucking pullets from the roost. I knew that while I slept or ran errands or sat alone at my books, Finnigan took Surrender to places he never intended to take me; I knew he told Surrender things he chose not to share with me. My feelings weren't hurt, not really — I told myself that Surrender was my dog and wherever he was, so was I; what he heard, I heard too. Besides, at that time and at that age, I had other things on my mind.

"Sarah!" I call. "Sarah!"

My nose has started to bleed.

She comes to the room after a short delay, dressed in

vulnerable cream. "Oh Gabriel!" she says. She bundles a towel against my face, tilts me forward and pinches my nose. These are such small things, but I can't do them myself. Anyway, I wanted her here. In this room the view never changes except as Sarah comes and goes.

While the bleeding slows she rubs my back, her fingers rumbling on my ribs. I want to say *Don't rub too hard*, for under the press of her hand I can feel my skeleton give. My bones are brittle, like those brought up from a desiccated tomb. Instead I shake myself free from the towel and say nothing of the sort. "Where were you?" I ask, accusingly.

"Working," she answers, looking surprised. "There's lots to do around here, you know."

" . . . Has anyone come around, asking for me?"

"No, Gabe."

"But if you were working, you might not have seen . . ."

She shakes her head slowly. "There's been no one, Gabriel."

I sink in my pillows, suck the blood from my lips.

"Who are you expecting?" She almost whispers it. I glance away. I won't tell.

Instead I ask feebly, "Can you stay with me?"

And she does; she changes my nightshirt and massages

my feet, she rubs lotion into my hands. She brushes my
hair and dabs oil on my lips, refreshes the linen on my
wounds. She does all this gladly, chatting away, yet I can
see her thoughts slip through the walls, I can hear her
wishing I'd go to sleep so she can get on with what occu-
pies her. But I stay vividly awake, watching her. I'll sleep
when I'm dead.

The year I was fifteen was the year my mother took to muttering under her breath when she encountered any young
lady who had even the vaguest potential to catch the eye
of a young man. She would stand at the window, ironing
clothes, curtained from sight, assessing passersby. Most of
them she dismissed with a sharp click of the tongue. But
if a girl of a certain age came along, Mother would mutter
as if laying a hex. Meeting such specimens in town made
her grimace, brisk her pace, shoo me onward, cast her
curse. In the evening, washing dishes, she would tally the
horrible total of faults she had encountered that day. *That
Jessica Flyte's got a face like a fish; someone should tell her
she's not all that she thinks. Deirdre Smythe will be fat, like
her mother. Lillian Brink's very la-di-da; I pity the man who
marries her.* And she'd drive them all off with hisses and

spits, the sound of an attacking reptile. I sensed from the start that this performance was for me, but for a time I couldn't guess its reason. It was in a moment when my mind was blank that I eventually understood. My mother was making an island of me.

It's strange: I remember the moment as one wouldn't forget a fall into arctic seas. Since childhood I'd been building a wall meant to protect me from the worst of the harm. In that moment of understanding, however, the wall quaked and near-fatally cracked. My stomach flipped, my scalp crawled, my mind reeled sickeningly. I gripped my chair and sat still, though my instinct was to rampage or flee. My mother had breached the wall and I stood knee-deep in a brackeny fluid that was seeping through the cracks. I fought to control myself, halt the slide, expel her from my head. Already a corner of my brain had been made black and sodden by her.

I walked around in a stupor for days, tormented by the broken wall, the leaking fluid, the mush in my brain that felt like a bruise and smelled of pond scum, an odor that oozed through my skin. Only Finnigan noticed my distraction, and he watched me incuriously while I struggled to explain. We were on the hill that overlooked the cattle yards where the two of us had made our pact, years ago. Surrender was hunting through blackberry and weed, flushing out hysterical birds. The shadows cast by the pine trees waltzed on the compacted earth. When I'd wrung out my troubles and sagged, feeling gouged, Finnigan exploded with laughter. He laughed till he spluttered, till his hyena eyes streamed. He fell limply across the earth and pummeled it with his fists. He dragged himself out of the dust and whimpered, "Go on, tell it again."

"It isn't funny."

"Yes it is. Tell me again."

I glared at him, my heart beating fast. A desperate chasm was breaking open in me; even Finnigan, my friend, couldn't understand. "Shut up," I growled. "Why don't you ever shut up?"

Finnigan was chortling. "Mush in your brain! You've got mush *for* a brain! Your mother's as mad as a hatter: what do you care what she says?"

I looked away, my face burning, slivers of flesh sliced from me. Surrender's snout was buried in undergrowth; Finnigan's hands crouched like spiders on the ground. I said, "This is different — I can't explain. She's taking things from me that I don't even have.

Ordinary things—liking someone, being married, living a normal life. She doesn't want me getting that. She's ruining everything before it starts. She doesn't want me *ever* to be happy."

I glanced at him; his face was blank; perhaps it was simply impossible for him to appreciate. His own life would never be like anyone else's—he had no use for normal or ordinary things. But I wasn't that way: I hankered to be like everybody else. I felt mortally alone and defeated. I said, "I always thought that, one day, I'd get free. I'd walk away and be free. But now I don't think I can. I'll never get this bruise out of my brain."

Finnigan looked up sharply. "Walk away where?" he asked. "Where would you go?"

"I don't know: somewhere. I can't stay here."

"But what about me? We had a pact! You swore! And anyway, what makes you think somewhere else would be different? You'd still be kooksville, wherever you went."

I bit my lip. He watched me as a crocodile watches an animal bending to drink. Finally I said, "Be quiet."

"I'm just saying—"

"Yes: stop saying it. You're missing the point." I got to my feet, brushed the dust from my knees, walked away across the fawn earth. "You don't understand. You never do."

He answered instantly. "You're wrong."

I could not resist: I looked back at him. He wasn't easy to find among the shadows, being dusky as something grown from the soil. His eyes were resting calmly on me. "You're not alone, Gabriel. You have me. As long as you stay here, you'll have me. There'll be no damage in your head, no bruising, no mush. Nothing will hurt. I'll keep it all out. I've done it before. It's always been us — you and me. In the house, you and me, against *them*. Remember?"

I stared at him, straining to see — in the shifting shade of the trees he vanished and vanished again. My heart fluttered, my blood streamed, there was a strange weightlessness to my bones. "Yes," I said, "I remember. I know." I knew he was dangerous and that I was endangered, that he was, like my parents, making a prisoner of me — yet he was also salvation: I wasn't alone. "I'll see you later," I said, and shambled down the hill, leaving Surrender to choose whether to follow or stay. I walked until the land flattened and the sale yards stood like a rib cage around me, deserted but for the crows. The wind had dropped; Surrender hadn't followed; there was now some peace in my mind. I leaned on a railing and wiped grit from my eyes. I knew that the worst of my life was over, that things would never be so bad. Finnigan was unruly, perhaps he was mad—nonetheless a surge of affection went through me for him. I loved him for all the things he knew about me—for things like my brainstorming mother—and equally for all the things he didn't know: for things like Evangeline.

FINNIGAN

McIllwraith has fallen asleep on the floor. His eyes shut like someone pulled a fuse in his head, and he slept. I left Surrender in the roof and came down closer. The Constable makes a small noise as he sleeps, as if some tiny creature who lives in his nose uses this time to re-arrange its nest.

Outside, finally, it's true night. No longer gray, but black. He looks innocent as a babe, lying there, as if he was sleeping the sleep of the just.

I have the wooden pike that I ripped from the ceiling beam. It is as long as my arm from elbow to wrist. When I put it down on the kitchen counter, it clunks. I poke around in the kitchen, looking for something to eat. In the refrigerator I find a bottle of beer kept cold for surprise guests. I'm a surprise guest, so I take the bottle and pick up the stake and sit cross-legged on the couch. I can smell the perfume of the notebook-lady, detect the odor of ink.

The room is warm, which I like. I haven't got penguin
feathers or a wolf's coat — winter's long, for me. A stuffy
room is luxury. I wish that I could stay.

I lay the spike across my lap and take a swig of beer.

McIllwraith breathes; I look down at him. If the sun
was shining above us, my shadow would pool on him.
His eyelashes touch my toes — that's how close I am.
Maybe, in his dream, he smells me, the mountains, the
snowy sky.

I think of the bones they found in the forest. Finger
bones, feet bones, backbones, skull. Underneath his skin,
McIllwraith has bones the same.

Now Eli, I say, I want you to listen. I'm not very happy
with you. . . . What's that? Why? What have you done?
Oh, I think you know. Remember how proud it made the
angel, to have you as a friend. He didn't have very many
friends — in fact, he had none. But he thought that he
had you.

McIllwraith is silent.

He trusted you. He ran big risks for you. Do you know
what his father would have done to him, if he'd found out
there was a traitor under his roof?

McIllwraith stays silent.

Nothing nice.

The beer bottle stings my hand, it's so cold.

But he was flattered and eager and honored to help you. And what thanks did you give? McIllwraith, answer me.

There's silence. Just the fire, a log falling.

You weren't his friend. You used him, that's all. And when you saw the chance to make a name for yourself, you used him again. You forgot all the things he'd done for you, all the risks he'd run. Now you've got perfumed ladies in your house; now your escape is at hand. And where is our angel? Shut up in a room.

McIllwraith shifts, nervously.

Now, I admire treachery as much as anyone. But I can't let it go unpunished. The angel might forgive you—that's his job. Not mine. So here I am: here we both are.

Put the stake away, Finnigan. Let's talk reasonably about this.

Don't tell me what to do, Eli. You know I can't bear that.

And before he can protest further, I put the stake away.

GABRIEL

I think it was her name that drew my attention. *Evangeline*: the word itself is holy.

In the center of my palms spread two dark lakes. They are not wounds—flesh ices them over. But the blackness is blood, gathered swampishly. When I press a finger to the fluid, it radiates. When I clamp and unclamp my fists, it dissipates. Slowly it refills, a little deeper each time, a little blacker, a swelling swamp. Such unnecessary reminders of my approaching fate irritate me no end. I drag words up my rusty throat and say to my body, "Look alive."

In a small town the generations are corralled like cows on market day: Evangeline was my generation, the twig of her family tree. I knew her parents and grandparents; I'd smiled and nodded at them. I knew her house, its white camellias, although I'd never been inside. Her family name was inscribed three times beneath the soldier who guarded the war memorial; a street planted with plane trees bore the same name. In the cemetery, a cherub cast a bulbous shadow across her great-great-granddad. I don't know if Evangeline gave this long lineage any thought — it was her inheritance from the cradle, so perhaps boring to her. But to me, who came from nowhere, whose family tree spread no further than a girl in a photograph, who glimpsed the future only through the sheenless prisms of my parents, Evangeline's history seemed a precious and extraordinary thing. I liked the way the sturdy branches of her tree lifted her up to the sun.

I had known her forever, as is the way in country towns. She and I had started school together as children, and traveled through it at a matching pace year after year. For most of those years we paid scarce attention to each other, and rarely spoke but to apologize for a knocked book or trodden toe. Evangeline's obliviousness was a reason to like her rather than not: I liked least those schoolfellows whose awareness of me invariably caused misery.

So I knew her, and always had, but we'd never had anything to say. She was popular; I was not. She came from a respected family; I, as Finnigan delighted to remind me, sprang from kooksville. In the lives of one another, we were like feathers—inconsequential; and other.

In the end I didn't even see her, but only heard: *Evangeline*.

I was gazing out the science-room window, my mind flat as a plain, and when the teacher barked her name a soft thought came drifting down on me. *Evangeline*, I thought: what a beautiful word.

I looked along the aisle and saw her, and it was as if I saw her for the first time. Everything changed. The ancient featureless interior of me spangled orange, mint, cat-blue. I looked back to the window immediately, my face damp, my breath caught. And worried I would never have the courage to look at her again.

The recollection of this is making me wheeze.

I don't want to go back there, through all of it. Affection makes fools. Always, without exception, love digs a channel that's sooner or later flooded by the briny water of despair. Back then, I didn't know this to be the fact I know it is now. But I knew enough to realize that I needed to take care; already, from the moment I heard her, I was working to minimize the harm. And the first safekeeping rule I made was this: do not tell.

Yet that very afternoon I saw Finnigan loitering in a lane, and as I came closer I saw that he already knew. He had guessed; he was laughing; I warned him sourly, "Don't say anything to her."

"Why not?" He laughed. "Won't you?"

Of course I would not. I knew my lowly rank. I pledged to keep, around Evangeline, a selfless silence, and suffered in it. It stung when we passed in the corridors; her voice would slice my skin. My eyes smarted at the sight of her sitting against a brick wall. A day spent in her vicinity left me exhausted: "Ain't love grand," said Finnigan.

One fateful day she caught me studying her; she quirked an eyebrow and glanced away. I blushed scarlet and stared at the tabletop, an oceanic roar in my ears. I was mortified—yet quietly pleased. I felt as if, after a long time's explaining, I had made myself understood. I wondered if she was looking at me, thinking about me, or if I'd dropped clean from her mind. Whichever it was would kill me. I was sixteen, and life wasn't simple.

The ocean in my ears parted. "Anwell!"

I looked up, empty-headed. The green glare of Volton, the English teacher, pinned me. He stood by the blackboard, chalk in hand. I'd seen this man in the supermarket, buying bulbs and frozen pies. My classmates turned to look at me, three rows of eager anticipation. In the stillness I heard the window rattle, the warble of a currawong. I groped for the unknown response to an unheard question. Had I been anybody else, someone would have come to my aid, muttering the answer at the cost of reprimand. But there was only silence, a slowly spinning white noise. "I'm sorry," I said. "I wasn't listening."

"What were you doing?"

The moment hung: "Thinking. I don't know."

"Thinking! Care to share your thoughts with us?"

I watched him. My desk was in a corner, tucked against the wall. Gray faces looked at me; some of them dumbly laughed. Many times I had seen Volton taking his morning constitutional around the town, followed boldly wherever he went by his slim black cat Tinker, whose collar was red, who shied at no thing. I knew where he lived and what he ate and I knew what was close to his heart. "No."

"Are you sure? I don't doubt they were fascinating. You were looking at Evangeline: have you something to say to her?"

Through death-throes I repeated, "No."

Volton tapped the chalk in his palm. "In my class you think about English, Anwell. The rest of it stays in your bedroom. Get it?"

The class burst like a firecracker, shrieking raucously. Morose and taciturn farmers' sons rocked in their chairs. The girls wriggled and squealed. The air rang with wolf-whistling; someone threw a paper plane. The teacher himself flashed me a smile, suggesting his persecution had meant no harm, suggesting, perhaps, that he'd done me a favor, making me appear the puerile equal of any other young man. He clapped his hands to quell the disorder and the class gave it up reluctantly, chuckles skimming the room. Volton returned to the blackboard and I cautiously raised my eyes. I made myself deaf and blind to everything but Volton. I watched him writing, strolling about, flipping through textbooks, speaking words. I watched his shoulders, his vulnerable neck; I watched the working of the tendons on which his lonely life hung. I did not look at Evangeline, and felt I never could again. In my mind was turning a single word: *rue*.

Later, when I told him this, Finnigan hooted like a drain.

For days, each breath I drew was quaky.

Disgraced, I saw my folly. I had tried to be like everyone else. I had seen my peers teased for their affections, seen them blush purple, heard the same catcalls, but sharing the experience didn't bring us closer. Rather, it stretched the distance between us. My excursion into their world had ended in humiliation, and resentment of my trespass. In the schoolyard a quiet melody followed me—"Evangeline! Evangeline!"—until the thing I'd loved, *Evangeline*, made my stomach clench.

I determined to restore my life to what it had been. In the corridors I kept my distance; in the classrooms I chose a seat far away. Always I kept my gaze steadfastly on the ground. If I heard her voice, I did not look up—my heart would beat urgently, but this I'd ignore. On the main street, if I saw her, I'd swing like a puppet through the nearest shop door. Walking Surrender around Mulyan, realizing her house was near, I would veer down one road, then another, roaming lostly on streets I'd always known. For weeks I was only eyes and ears, scanning for her, listening, ignoring my heart's flutter, chewing my fingernails. And as the weeks passed, the wounds I'd received began to heal, though they left behind ropy scars. At school I could look up from the linoleum; I could share the supermarket with her. I saw that, one day, things could once again be as they'd always been.

Finnigan watched all this through amused eyes. The mere mention of her name made him cackle. "I hope you've learned your lesson," he said, sounding just like my mother.

Then one Saturday morning at the start of the holidays I was on my knees in the backyard when I heard her say, "Anwell?"

My heart stopped.

She was standing at the wire gate that marked the line between our yard and a public lane. The lane was forested with weeds and overgrown with briar; it was a shortcut to Mulyan's shops and Evangeline carried a carton of milk. But her house stood on the other side of town — the lane wasn't a shortcut to anywhere, for her. The reason she stood there was me.

Surrender was pacing at the gate, staring up at her. He had not barked, and his tail swept slowly; I wondered how long she'd been there. I didn't stand up — I didn't know what she wanted. I wondered if her friends were watching from the shadows that hulked across the lane. A bead of sweat went down my back. Finally I said something. "Hello."

She reached a hand over the gate and stroked the dog's head. "Hello, Surrender."

It felt like a punch, that she knew his name. She scratched his ear, and the dog's tail waved. She glanced across the grass to where I crouched imprisoned against the earth. I stared at her, transfixed. Distantly I prayed that Mother wasn't at the kitchen sink, where the view through the window ducked the arbor and stretched down the lane.

And Finnigan, I begged, *Keep away*.

Evangeline said something, her voice coasting the grass. "What are you hiding?"

I was using my T-shirt to hammock a small creature and I looked down at it, stupefied. In a moment she was going to walk away, wondering why she'd bothered; she would not come again. I gathered my thoughts and said, "Shut your eyes."

She looked surprised; then she smiled, leaned the milk against the gate, and closed her eyes trustingly. I gathered the creature inside my shirt, stood up, and crossed the lawn. Bees and a single dragonfly flew up, from the grass. As I drew closer I could smell her, lilac. "Hold out your hands."

She did so, the smile slung on her lips, sunlight tilting on her hair. Her hands made a creviced cup lined with ten bitten crescent-moons. Around her left wrist swayed a silver chain—I had noticed it before. To see it in such detail stung my eyes. "Don't be afraid," I said.

"I'm not."

Her teeth weren't perfect: I liked that. "I won't hurt you."

"I believe you."

I scooped up the creature and placed it in her hands. My knuckles brushed her fingertips. The creature blinked black beads at me; it did not pipe or struggle. "All right," I said, "you can look."

Evangeline opened her eyes. The duckling was yellow as buttercup, fluffy as snowflakes; its wings were twin butterfies. She caught her breath, couldn't think what to say. She and I, Surrender and the duckling, the roses, the weeds, the sky, the trees: she looked at me and laughed like a bell. "Beautiful," she said. "How beautiful, Anwell."

I went to laugh with her, went to say something— and stalled. I suddenly remembered our audience in the shadows, the laughter rollicking round the classroom. My stomach pitched; I stepped back. Evangeline glanced up from the duckling. "Everyone reckons Mr. Volton is an idiot," she said. "I just wanted to tell you that."

I trod on my toes and almost tripped. Evangeline had already looked away. She stroked the duckling with the tip of her thumb. Her nose was powdered with freckles, her ears pierced with many silver hoops. "His heart's broken now, though. His cat's disappeared."

". . . Tinker?"

"Yes; poor thing. He loved that cat. He walks around calling for it. He's put notices in all the shop windows."

I said, "I haven't seen it."

"No, it's long gone." She shrugged, her eyes on the duckling, which, grown restless, was struggling in her palm. "I suppose that's what happens when you make other people's lives miserable: life gets miserable back at you."

She, too, had suffered on that day: I said, "I'm sorry, Evangeline."

She smiled gracefully. "You don't have to be. It doesn't matter. Stupid things like that don't matter, Anwell."

A bird called; I could look away.

She said, "I'm thinking of walking up Rabbit Road. Want to come?"

Once more I stalled—I admit I was afraid. Of my mother, my father, what Finnigan would say. As the moment skipped by, Evangeline added, "No one else is going—only me. Maybe Surrender."

"OK," I said. And felt a keen freedom doing so; I would have been a fool to do otherwise.

"I'll take the milk home. Then I'll meet you at the end of the lane." She looked up at the sky. "Will it rain?"

I glanced at the cloudless, heat-bleached sky. "No."

"Hmm. If it rains we'll go anyway. All right?"

"All right." I smiled; it seemed funny. She passed the duckling over the gate. Again, her fingers touched mine.

"See you later," she said.

I watched her stride down the lane, the carton of milk swinging at her knees; she did not look back or wave. At the end of the lane she rounded the corner and disappeared, leaving only the smudge of flattened grass by the gate to prove that the morning was real.

Surrender yawned and lay at my side, and for the first time in centuries I breathed.

I open my eyes. There is noise.

"Sarah?"

The door to my room stays marmishly shut. But nonetheless there's noise. There shouldn't be any noise in this town that holds a requiem-hush for me.

I glance, confused, around the room.

Maybe — it could be — I whisper it: "Evangeline?"

I wait, my heart thumping. Moments pass, the noise goes on. Now I know it's not her. "Sarah!"

To raise my voice always makes me cough. I rasp and splutter, curl up like a worm. My vision swims with tears. Colors spangle the window—it's dark outside, yet there's color. There's what sounds like commotion. "Sarah!" I roar, furious now.

The door opens, my aunt hurries in. "Gabriel, I'm sorry!" She says it like she means it. Cool air has come in with her. She skirts the bed and pours water.

"What's happening?" I ask, although I know.

Sarah doesn't look up. The glass fills. I see her hand is shaking a little, that the glass is not held still. "What do you mean? Nothing's happening."

She's lying. "There's lights," I say. "There's noise."

"It's nothing special," she insists. "Nothing, as far as I know."

I gaze coolly at her. There's no point arguing. I know what the light is, and the color.

It is fire.

It's Finnigan.

FINNIGAN

There's fire in my fingers. I burn everything I touch.

Lights are on in Gabriel's house. It's been a while since I was here. Everything looks the same in the feather-red light. The building is wood, painted cream. Across the garden stands the fence where years ago I carved my name. The angel treated the scratchings like a holy relic. His only proof of me. I was so often tempted to scrub the letters off. After a while, the weather did it for me. Now there's no word, no name, no proof, just the fence.

I put my fiery hands in my pockets, walk away from the crackling light. Cross the lawn to where the night's gathered black as mortal sin. Surrender, the dark's dog, follows me. We sit down with our spines to the wall.

I look up. See the gutter. The stars, the moon, the smoke.

From somewhere an alarm starts howling. I fold my hand round Surrender's muzzle .so he cannot join the song.

We're sitting against the wall of the house and above us there's a window with a curtain and four bars. Beyond the window is the angel. He must know that we are here.

I will slip a wrist between the bars and when I run my fingers down the glass, the sound will be . granite screaming.

GABRIEL

Time is shorter than I'd thought: very well. I haven't seen
Finnigan for more than a year. It seems longer than that.
This small room irked him when he was last here; my
weakness infuriated him. He'd urged me to get up and
walk. He'd flirted with Sarah and been rude to the doctor.
I'd had to ask him to leave. He'd done so in black temper,
and I knew that one day he'd return.

Sarah has shut the door behind her, but that won't slow
him down. I whisper an incantation that's both protection
and welcome. I can hear an alarm's piercing wail. I can
hardly hear myself think.

We walked side-by-side up the steep flank of Rabbit Road,
me edgy as a hare until the scrub stood between us and
anybody who might see; though I simmered with pride to
be with her, I dreaded the consequences of being seen.
Any of Mulyan's young men might take offense at my

filling a place better occupied by them; anyone, seeing me, might mention it to my mother and father. Each snapping twig made my heart leap; each rolling pebble chilled my blood. I kept my eyes on the peak. Though she talked, I couldn't listen. It was a relief to reach the peak, where we shrank to smaller than specks. Overlooking green gullies and the forest's canopy, Evangeline rolled cigarettes and we sat, not together, but with a companionable closeness. In the small sahara of earth between us I piled stones and listened, saying little. Evangeline, like Finnigan, talked of the future. Her eyes on the grizzled tip of her cigarette, she told me that she worried she would never leave Mulyan, that the only horizons in her life were the icy horizons of our mountain range, that her world would be contained in the view from the dead end of Rabbit Road. I said, "If you stayed here forever, it wouldn't be wrong. It wouldn't stop you living a good life."

She looked through cat tails of smoke. "You think?"

"Life is lived on the inside. What's outside doesn't matter."

She thought about this, her cigarette pluming. It prickled my skin, knowing my words were in her head. She waved away the smoke and asked, "What's inside you?"

The question bothered me, I glanced away. I glimpsed my elbows, my jutting kneecaps. What was inside me. I felt conscious of it. "Colors, maybe."

"Colors! Which ones?"

"Blue." Blood pulsed through my fingers; I was aware of my feet, the size of my hands. Everything worked smoothly. "Green."

"Hmm. Nice colors."

I nodded; I had hardly dared to look at her, not during the climb up the road, not now while we sat on the rocks. I was conscious of my skin, my teeth, my blowing hair. In my wrists was a matchbox collection of bones. She leaned on the hand that had no cigarette. "Colors," she said. "I wouldn't have guessed. I see you every day, Anwell, but I don't know anything about you. I wonder why we weren't friends before."

Later that day, I told Finnigan she'd said that. "I wonder why we weren't friends before." It seemed like a compliment. Finnigan giggled with unpleasant mirth. "*I wonder why we weren't friends before.* Did you tell her," he answered, "that you don't want to be friends? Did you tell her you've already got a friend?"

He was perched in a birch tree, as if he'd flown there. It was early evening and the low sun blinded me. I stared up at him, anger blowing like a banner. He had much and I had little, yet still he'd spoil it for me. "Stay out of it," I warned. "You stay away."

Finnigan twitched a branch, an arboreal shrug. He was black and white as a lemur. "All I'm saying is you'd better be careful. You better remember she only wants to be friends."

I swung away. "You're being ridiculous."

"If you won't listen, don't come crawling later. Maybe I'll be gone."

"Yeah, yeah. Don't make empty threats."

"Have I ever, Gabriel?"

I stopped, and looked back. A tornado of midges was swirling round the birch. From somewhere came the cobbly sound of a horse trotting on a road. "You can't change the rules, Finnigan. We made a promise. Like reflections and blood brothers—remember? You promised to be here when I need you."

"I remember," he said. "But I was lying."

I stared at him; he lounged in the leaves and looked smug at me. I could have shaken him from the boughs and clubbed him. His clothes hung in rags, his hair was filthy. He looked leaner, more sinewy, than ever; he was brown and stained, but his eyes shone, as always, with a ruby brilliance; from his face the hyena smiled. There was no point arguing with him in this mood. The setting sun washed the lawn orange and lemon; the scent of roses turned in the air. A cicada scraped its wings. From the chicken coop I felt the study of pale, thoughtless eyes. "Where's Surrender?"

"Who knows. He's feral, that dog. Won't come when he's called, won't do what he's told."

I said nothing; I longed to be gone. I wanted to be somewhere on my own, to reflect in private on this long day. This morning I had knelt in the grass with a duckling, and everything had been the same; now, at dusk, nothing was. "I'll find him."

"Why? He doesn't want you to. I think you should leave him alone."

"He's my dog," I retorted. "Not yours."

Finnigan didn't flinch. But as I walked away he said, "You lied too."

Against my instincts I looked back.

He was upside-down like a monkey, swinging. "You lied to Evangeline. You said you liked her, but you still lied."

I should have kicked him in the stomach, trampled him into the earth; I could feel his will to undermine and disconcert me. "What do you mean?"

He grinned, lopsided, gruesomely. "The colors were never blue and green. The colors are soot and pearl."

I put my hands over my ears and just walked away.

If I could have my life over again I'd want back just those few weeks of summer. Not a minute longer — not a moment of Finnigan in the birch tree, not a moment of the day I would soon spend in the forest while the world imploded around me. No, just these few weeks in between. They weren't perfect — I was anguished and edgy, and plagued by doubt. But at least, for their duration, I was alive.

A small town has as many eyes as a fly; Evangeline became the secrecy around which my existence turned. No one must know; vitally, my mother mustn't. Sometimes I would lie in a sweat, tormented by visions of what would happen if she discovered the truth. I never invited Evangeline to the house; inside it, I never mentioned her name. I did not look out the window if she was walking by. I pretended nothing had changed. But, in my head, she'd become a vast choppy sea that drowned out all other things. I closed my books, overlooked Surrender, chewed my nails to the quick. For hours at a time I gave Finnigan no thought. I was distracted, morose, feverish, vacant, I felt I lived in some pleasantly maddening cage, where my thoughts could roam but never beyond her. My father observed I was moping like a fool; my mother leveled on me an insect stare and decided, "It's his age. It's a foolish age."

Father said, "I wasn't foolish at his age."

I have defied you, I itched to tell them: though you'd make it otherwise, I am just like anyone else; like anybody should do, I've reached a foolish age. Of course I said nothing, and was proud to hold my tongue, because I didn't *want* Evangeline's name spoken inside the house, didn't want it dragged across the floor. Only secrecy shielded her from my mother and father; only in secrecy could she remain pristine.

I struggled to find ways of explaining this to her— finally I realized I could save my breath. Evangeline never tried to take my hand. She never suggested that we sit together in the rotunda or walk arm-in-arm along the street. She never asked to come to the house, never telephoned and left a message for me. She didn't invite me to join herself and her friends when they went swimming in the river or day-tripped to a neighboring town. She would smile at me if we passed in the street, she would not say my name. She was content to exist on the fringes. We circled each other's lives like moons.

GABRIEL

We met among trees and on the edges of fields and by the creek where ebony snakes slid under stones; it suited us to meet this way, in wild places, like migrating birds. We never arranged our meetings — sometimes days would go by and I wouldn't see her. Then I'd round a corner and there she would be, slouched smoking, as if waiting, and I would stop and talk to her. "It's funny how we find each other," I told Finnigan. "It's fate."

"It's not funny," he replied. "It's not fate. You're following her around."

"What? I'm *not!*"

"You are. You're the hunter and the gatherer. You're the lurker-in-the-shade. You're the symphony of stalking—"

"It's a small town!"

"Yeah, a small town. Nowhere to hide. Nowhere to hide, except in a crowd."

Air hissed past my teeth. That morning Evangeline and I had passed in the park. Neither of us was alone. My father was tweaking the leaves of the roses there, accusing them of spreading black-spot across town. Evangeline walked by, accompanied by two friends. They gave us a wide berth. I knew their names, and they all knew mine, but none of us said anything, I kept my eyes down, and Evangeline continued the tale she was telling her friends.

149

She was louder and more frivolous with them than with me. To Finnigan I said, "You know I can't talk to her in public. You know what people — what my parents — would say. My life is already hard, Finnigan: why do you try to make it worse? What terrible thing have I done to you?"

Like a fox he looked at me. He said, "You shut me in a refrigerator."

I staggered. "What?"

He barked with laughter and swirled away. "Gabriel, take a joke!"

If I had the chance to live again those few weeks of the summer I was sixteen I would exorcise from them these miserable spats with him; I would strip them of everything except the dawns and midnights and the hours I spent alone with Evangeline: the summer, thus experienced, would be without flaw. Sometimes I would invite her on rambling walks, and if she was doing nothing else then she'd sometimes follow me. She would slap her pockets for her tobacco and as we walked she would smoke one cigarette while rolling another. I knew places where nobody went, and our walks would take us there. We scaled the peak of McAlister's Bluff, where Jaffy Avalon the shape-changer discovered it took more than faith in one's shape-changing talents to make wings out of bare arms.

We followed the disused railway tracks, Evangeline balanced on the rails, until the tracks became crusty with rust and disintegrated into the soil. We picked blackberries and ate them, though neither of us liked the taste. One balmy dusk we climbed the junkyard fence and wandered among life's leftovers, stoves, billycarts, wild cats, chunks of wall, and Evangeline, hands on hips, surveyed everything and decided, "This is where you'd dump a body."

"You think so?"

"Don't you?"

"No."

Summer lit the world.

We walked into the forests that encircled the town. I have never liked them, their dark throat, their sullen height, their slump-shouldered gloom. But Evangeline walked steadily into their maw, and I followed her. She wanted to see the swathes which, years ago, the firebug had burned. The furnaced forest was green again, though here and there stood leafless trunks cindered to the core; on the scruffy dirt lay stiff black limbs tangled in morning glory. Evangeline touched her palm to the charcoal, murmured, "Poor things."

I scanned the treetops for Finnigan. I never felt closer to him than when I trespassed on his territory. Dark and dirty, sulky, oppressive, he was like a creature that the leaves and creaking timber had spawned. I never saw him, but I felt observed. He scoffed, "Watch you mooching after her like a mutt — why would I waste my time?" It didn't make me believe him. He shrugged, unconcerned. "It's not me you need to worry about, Gabriel."

This I knew, believed.

I was careful not to give my parents reason to ask where I'd been or where I was going or any questions at all; I was careful not to give them any cause for complaint. I distilled the charms of angelhood; I oozed meek compliance. I re-membered how, as a child, I'd tried to build a wall of good behavior behind which Vernon and I might hide: I could never make the wall strong enough; it was forever toppling and leaving us exposed. Now I was older, and had Evangeline to protect: I could try harder. I did my chores efficiently and without being told. I cleaned, shopped, washed, swept. I cut firewood and, from my empire of chickens and ducks, selected, once a fortnight, the unfortunate who would taste the ax. I'd deliver Mother's supper to her room, then take a place opposite my father at the blood-dark din-ing table. Father rarely spoke while we ate, and certainly never mentioned his legal work, which he deemed me too unimaginative to comprehend. Imagine it, however, I did;

I thought of the hours he spent settling divorces and selling farms and drawing up wills. I thought of all the hours behind him and all the hours to come, the boredom of it, the sameness. I imagined him at his aerie window, overseeing the town. In his spare time he continued a desultory campaign against McIllwraith, unable to abandon it for fear of appearing defeated or proven wrong—he took great sport in reminding the townsfolk that the arsonist had never, in fact, been caught. A proud man, he refused to acknowledge his alienation from the world. He made no comment on his crumpled home life. He ignored the silence that descended when he entered any room. He kept company with his roses and steadfastly believed that everything was as it should be.

My mother's world had contracted like a dying spider.

In the past year she had become isolated, and increasingly querulous. Her days of stalking the town had ended, and she kept to the house and yard. She'd come to feel that Mulyan was an ungrateful place, its inhabitants not worth the effort. She wafted whitely through the rooms, bored, alert to insults, alone. She went nowhere and spoke to no one. I felt instinctively that her hibernation could end at any time, that she was banking energy for the moment she chose to rise and return. I understood that,

GABRIEL

although she lived in rooms, the world—*my* world—lay at her feet, shielded from her sight by something flimsy as silk. Mother need simply twitch the hem, and the truth would be revealed. My mother was like an adder in an unlocked cage.

I read to her; I didn't complain. I did exactly as I was told.

I shut the windows against laughter on the street.

In our house, the floors and walls were ice.

Within the house I never so much as whispered Evangeline's name. I thought of her, I ached with worry that I was missing a chance to talk with her . . . but I would stay home, mute and harrowed, rather than raise suspicion and leave. If Mother called me, if Father wanted a pot of tea, I needed good reason not to be near and obey. On countless occasions I announced that I was going to walk the dog—only to find that Surrender was not in the yard, was off gallivanting somewhere with Finnigan. I couldn't disappear with a dog that was gone. Frustrated, I berated Finnigan: "Don't blame me," he replied. "Surrender follows because he wants to—I don't make him."

I gritted my teeth. "Make him stay in the yard."

"I won't."

"Then I'll chain him up. That will stop him."

Finnigan lifted his gaze and laid it coldly on me. "You're your father's son, aren't you."

That quieted me. It was minutes before I could look up from the stones. I stroked the dog's canoe-brown head, ran a hand across the soft peaks of his mountain-range shoulders. He needed chaining—in the past I'd seen gore on his paws, wool snagged in his teeth—but, "Yes," I sighed. "I'm sorry."

He should see me now, that addict of hurt, that merchant of distress: I'm paying for my sins. Now I hardly sleep, and exhaustion eats at me; I'm jerked from rare, merciful moments of rest by goblins gouging my chest. Now my throat constricts around clots of mortality so I struggle in panic to breathe. Now I couldn't cross the room without help; now I'm almost too weak to blink. Now, undrugged, I am nothing but ache.

This is the price: it's high. I close my eyes and want never to open them again. I want somebody to tell me, *You needn't open them again.*

The drip needle is like a talon in my wrist. My arm is lame with the pain. If I could, I would peel from my skin the tape that holds the needle in place and I'd draw the spike from my vein. I wouldn't want it leaking its fluids onto the floor, so I would drop the tube into the water jug. It would coil and float there like a glass worm.

If I could, I would do it.

I could ask Finnigan, when he gets here, but he'll refuse.

Once more, then, to close my eyes.

In the end I suppose I walked with her only six or seven times; I suppose we only spoke for a handful of hours. It's funny how, in my head, everything seems larger. I counted the smiles she gave me, the turns of her head. I remember the grain of the sunshine on the carved nape of her neck. "What do you talk about?" Finnigan asked once, although surely he knew.

I lay in the warm grass, my heart shuddering with joy. To be in love is so exciting. "Things. School. People. Nothing."

"Vernon?"

"A little."

"You've dragged him out for her entertainment?"

". . . No, it's not like that."

And I hoped it wasn't.

"Do you talk about me?"

The sky was bluer than I'd ever seen. I reached up

and wrapped my fingers around a cloud. I was stalling, pretending I wasn't afraid. "You know I don't like to talk about you."

"Why not? I'm not important?"

I folded my hand to my chest, felt my heart beating there. "You said no one would believe me if I told them about you. You also said you would kill me if I ever told."

"That was child talk."

"I believed you, though."

He set his jaw. I buried my sights in the grass, saw ants dragging a dead cricket. Here, at the ragged edge of the creek, where weeds and scraps of rubbish thrived, the trees grew green and quiet. The water moved slickly over moss-covered rocks; apart from the whir of click-bugs in the leaves, the only sound was Surrender's panting. Finnigan stared at me with his predator eyes; I had to say something or die. "I like you being my secret. I don't want to share."

He licked his lips, looked away. I drew an unrelieved breath. We both knew that what I said was the truth, as well as being a lie. The pure and honest answer was pinging between us, hovering above the weeds. Neither of us reached to catch it. Finnigan sighed, brushed hair from his eyes. His hair was long now, and incorrigibly matted. Always scruffed around the edges, on this day he looked particularly shabby. His elbows were crusted with dirt, his hands marked with inflamed nicks, the legacy of a tangle with barbed wire. He looked hungry, untended, adrift. A brook of sadness suddenly welled in me, at the thought of the hard life he led. To break the unhappy silence I said, "We talk about nothing, Fin — nothing that would interest you. We talk about my mother and father. We talk about how things are, for me. About how to change things. It's just my life, Finnigan — stupid things."

He watched me wave a hand, indicating my entire faulty world. He said, "You're telling her everything that's important. Everything she can laugh about later, with her friends."

I did not flinch. "She wouldn't."

"How do you know? How do you know? You hardly know her."

"I trust her," I said. "That's why."

"Do you trust me? I've known you forever."

"I know. I do. I do trust you."

He gazed at me. Midges blew past his eyes. "You liar," he said, and chuckled.

* * *

From the swirling depths to which I've sunk I hear footsteps in the hall. I open my eyes, consider the ceiling.
My breathing hardly disrupts the sheet. The footsteps
come, without hurry; the floorboards complain. Finnigan,
it seems, has chosen the most untriumphant way to return. He could have slipped down the chimney or crashed
in a window, he could have smashed through the ceiling
or ripped a hole in the floor. Instead he walks peacefully,
something tame.

My eyes grate like sandpaper in their sockets. I turn
my head and rest my chin on the pillow. Now I can see
the door.

The footfalls stop. Maybe the clock in the dining room
does too, there's such a cavernous silence.

In this room, night is not black but gray. The door is
gray, the walls are gray, the air itself is gray. Yet light skates
goldenly round the door handle as it spins.

I remember vividly the last hot afternoon. Surrender,
Finnigan, and I were wedged in the space between
the chicken coop and the back fence. Sunshine never
reached this place, nor did very much rain. Feathers could
lie here for years, unblown; spider webs, decades old,
hung preserved. Snapstick, indifferent to conditions,

covered the earth with a maze of green stem, and had raised pink welts on our arms. The fence line was potholed with burrows; the fence itself bowed drunkly. A shower of paint rained from the coop wall when Surrender stretched and restlessly moved. It was a dry, windless day, and our closeness made us irritable. Finnigan could talk of only one thing—nothing else concerned him anymore. "Surrender doesn't like her," he was saying, his voice like a bee. "You don't like her, do you, Surrender?"

I had my shoulders against the fence and my heels propped on the coop. I was smoking a cigarette, though this wasn't my habit. The smoke whittled up the wall but dispersed when it reached open air. "He doesn't have to like her."

Finnigan sneered, radiating petulance. He picked his teeth with a twig of snapstick, his gaze skimming loose and dangerous. He reached out to take the dog's paw. The dog glanced at the hyena and apprehensively away. "Do you know what else?" Finnigan asked, in a voice sweet and unearnest. "Do you know what else, Surrender? The girl doesn't like the boy."

I plucked the cigarette from my lips. "Shut up, Finnigan. You don't know anything about it."

Finnigan smiled affectionately at the dog. "We know some things, don't we, Surrender? We know most things, in fact. We know—for instance—that Evangeline's got a lot of friends—hasn't she, my hound? Yes. She goes with them to the pictures and driving up the road. She doesn't do that with Gabriel. How come? Is she ashamed to be seen with him? Maybe."

"That's not why!" I struggled to sit up, a brittle storm of paint shedding from the coop. "I wish you'd mind your own business!"

Finnigan squeezed Surrender's paw, gazed steadfastly into the dog's eyes. "I think Evangeline should get herself a *proper* boyfriend, don't you, Surrender? One she's not embarrassed to show off in public. But oops, I forgot— Gabriel's *not* her boyfriend, is he? Gabriel is only her *friend.*"

I felt a giddy sickness rising, and a tide of crushing shame. "You don't know anything," I breathed. "I wish you'd stay out of it—"

But Finnigan continued blithely, as if he hadn't heard. "Only a *friend,*" he marveled, "and she's *still* embarrassed to be seen with him! I wonder why she bothers? Maybe because . . . well, she's got everything, hasn't she? Nice house, nice family, nice little friends. Now she's got Gabriel, her nice little kook. Her nice little locker-in-the-refrigerator. Not everyone's got one of those, have they! He's a well-trained pet, too: he runs and jumps and sighs for her. He walks and talks and pants for her. Would you do that for me, Surrender? Would you? No — you've got too much pride."

He uncurled his claws from around the dog's paw and stroked the animal's ear. I glared at the wall, hating him massively inside. Finnigan pressed his lips to the dog's head, murmured into the dense fur. "And what does the angel get in return, hound? Nothing, I think. Gabriel's giving himself away, and he gets nothing back. Unless you count his dreams, of course, and all his wishful thinkings."

I shrank against the fence, mortified. It was true I couldn't bring myself to touch her, though it was all I wanted to do, all I could think about doing, the single thing I would die to do. My nights were filled with seared imaginings — my hand on her chest, my palm on her spine. I loved and dreaded the fanciful nights; the hammered day was better because she was there, a thousand times worse for the same reason. Again and again I vowed to reach out, and helplessly lost my nerve. I worried she would duck from beneath the weight of my uninvited touch; I worried, worse, that she would endure it with an ill-disguised shudder. I worried she would smile politely and murmur, *Anwell, don't.*

The humiliation of that would ruin everything, kill our friendship in its tracks. I told myself I would rather keep my hands to myself. Then changed my mind, knotted with anguish, then changed my mind again. I didn't know how to tell if somebody wanted to be touched, and I had no courage to take a chance. Staring down at my empty hands, I realized something I hadn't understood before. Never having been touched, I didn't know how to touch; such things would never come naturally to me.

I never felt my wrongness more keenly than I did in the dry weeks of the summer I was sixteen. I was frantic with indecision, with fear and desire. I didn't know how to make Evangeline like me. And I was deeply unsure about what to do next, in the unlikely event that she did.

And Finnigan knew.

I pressed to the fence, the air a snake around my neck. I said, "Finnigan, you were supposed to be my friend."

"You decided that. I never said that word."

"You are crushing me—"

"No—I'm telling you truth. I'm saving you."

I looked at him, my blood churning; he looked back, unmoved. Behind his peeling lips I saw a sliver of teeth.

"You're her game, Anwell," he said. "You're a strange little beetle she's put inside a jar. She'll keep you until she gets bored. Then she'll forget you, let you starve. Maybe she'll do something worse — maybe she'll feed you to the cat. And you know *why* she'll do this, Anwell? Because you're just a bug. Who can you complain to? How can you make her sorry? You can't — you can't do a thing. Mulyan is her town, not yours. No one here will take your side — they wouldn't even know they could, she's kept you such a secret. She can tell her friends you're dreaming, you're lying, and they'll believe her. After all, she's never been seen with you. She's never even said your name."

I looked at the dirt, at the trampled snapstick leaking fluid from its wounds. He shifted against the chicken coop, glanced up at the blue sky. "I think this, Anwell: I think she *does* like you — I think she thinks you're a pretty little beetle. But that's all you are. You're not a bright future for her. She'll ditch you in exchange for some boy — some farmer's son, some plumber — someone who isn't so *other*. Someone respectable. Someone who doesn't live in a jar. She *has* to do it, you see? She has to make her life good. That's what people want to do. So end it here and now, Anwell. Get rid of her, before she laughs at you. Before she hurts you to make you go away."

I stayed silent for moments. "You're mistaken," I said.

His face darkened. "Think again."

"No," I said. "I won't. I'm not like you, Finnigan. The water and trees and the hills . . . that's not enough for me. Maybe I am a bug in a jar—better that, than nothing. I'd rather be that, something alive—better than being a stone on the ground, like you."

The sky above our heads dashed white with cockatoos. Calmly as snow Finnigan said, "Think again, Gabriel."

I hit the earth with defiant fists. "No!" I shouted. "I won't! I don't belong to you! Don't tell me what to do!"

His black pool eyes looked into me. "You do belong to me," he said, "and I don't share."

He got to his feet, slapped his thigh for the dog. I felt delirious, desperate, aghast. The air swilled and cracked with peril. "Where are you going?" I asked. "What are you going to do?"

"There's only one thing I can do."

"What—you're leaving? You're abandoning me?"

His hand was on the top of the fence—in a moment he would leap and be gone. He cast me a dismissive glance and only answered, "You wish."

FINNIGAN

Open your eyes. Gabriel. Open your eyes.

I know he isn't asleep.

I fold my arms: I can wait.

This room hasn't changed since I was last here. It is square; it is white. The floor is checkered in ivory and ash. The bed frame is silver, the metal smoothly curved. A curtain covers the window. From the ceiling hangs a lightbulb bubbled by a plastic shade. Beside the bed stands a glittering spike, the skeleton of a crane. The spike holds a pouch that bulges with liquid. A tube runs from the pouch to a needle that's buried in the angel's right arm.

This is what he looks like: a creature hardly there. His face is gaunt, the skull showing through; his skin is bloodless and blue. His face is white as a lamb's.

His hair is longer than it used to be. It was once the color of roadside sand—now it's the same as the moon.

Locks of it curl like snail shells round his chin. His chest doesn't lift, as far as I can see. I can't hear him breathing.

He's not much more than a collection of bones. I see sockets, clavicle, wrists. The nightshirt must cover nothing but gristle and rib cage. I've never seen a living thing so lean. In this bone town, he could be prince. He is a disgusting sight.

Gabriel!

I know he hears.

Some things about him are the same as ever. He still looks painfully angelic. His lips still have a sore, swollen look to them, as if they've been hit with a bottle.

There's an antiseptic smell in the room. Also: trepidation. Also: me.

Finally he opens his eyes. Their color's the same — gasoline-blue.

You look like you've seen a ghost, I say; he smiles and says, *Finnigan.*

G A B R I E L

He looks the same as he always did. As if he can bend the world to his will.

It's not like seeing an old friend; nor is it like encountering an enemy. His year of absence slips away — it's as if I saw him yesterday. He's brought to the room his unforgotten smell. My blood feels warmer with recognition.

He shrugs off a coat that he's stolen from somewhere, and sits on the end of the bed. The weight feels strange and unpleasant, I think the bed pitches like a boat. I shift my hands as much as I'm able, wrap my fingers around the bed's frame. He watches this, my nerviness, and smiles. The hyena is still there in him — he's still single-minded, sole of purpose. He still has darkness around the eyes. He says, "You don't look good."

I answer, "You do."

And he does, which surprises me. I had thought that, without me, he would somehow fade. We blink at each other, smile, say nothing: inside the room there's silence but for the sigh of the sheets. Outside, however, the disquiet continues—the crackle of flames, the flaring of light, the rags of passing conversation. Finnigan taps his fingers on the bed. "You heard about the bones," he says.

". . . Yes, I did."

"That's why I'm here."

"Yes, I realize."

Our silence resumes. Finnigan's gaze coasts the water jug, the cupboard, the undecorated walls. He notes the tray that catches my cough and the cloths that soak up the blood. He looks at the bruise that the needle has raised. He twitches, as if for a twinlike moment he experiences pain. He looks at me and I see he's uncharacteristically perturbed. Abruptly he says, "Surrender's outside."

"Oh?"

"Want me to call him?"

"He's your dog," I say. "Do what you like."

Surrender was always more free than I. Neither of us owned our lives, but Surrender's freedom lay in not knowing it. Surrender knew no laws; to him, the world was a place made to give him room to run. The short balmy nights of summer were lit by stars underneath which he raced. Nights brought out foxes to harass, possums to bail up in trees; they stir-crazied the mad-eyed feral cats, which, lawless like himself, were wisely left alone. The sultriness of night drugged the hens, which teetered dazedly in their coops; it made horses and heifers skittish, and easy to stampede. Best of all, the nights' heat made the fat sheep sluggish, and slow to get to their feet. My own life lived in shackles, I could not bring myself to chain the dog—not when he came home with wool in the buckle of his collar, not when he yawned and showed rooster feathers snagged between his canines. Finnigan accused me of hypocrisy, I who'd vowed always to do what was right and proper. I sighed *I know it*, and my intentions were good, but still the chain lay unused in the grass. I did not say that while Surrender roamed at liberty, so did some shadow of myself: that the dog brought home stories of all he'd sniffed, heard, and seen, his dusty coat and road-sore paws telling cavalier tales of wit and piracy that widened the world for me. I'd pick the burrs and dandelion seeds from his coat, brush out the muck from cow fields, patch his many battle wounds. Free, he was enviably, brightly alive; through him, so was I.

I knew, inside, that I was walking the road to grief, but still I couldn't bring myself to chain him.

A dog that kills is also killed. It's a fact of life. Still I didn't use the chain.

A tethered thing is a dead thing, anyway.

I know it was he who broke into the coop of our neighbor Tutter down the road. A fox got the blame for that, but there was bird blood on my dog's paws. And the morning after I argued with Finnigan between the ramshackle fence and the chicken shed, Surrender brought home a small slain piglet, which I buried in a race against the sun, which rose unstoppably, like a vengeful spirit, to expose the crime. "Surrender," I whispered, "be careful," but the dog was already sleeping on the lawn, worn out by his escapades.

The first few days after he'd jumped the fence and gone, I'd kept an eye out for Finnigan. He had departed in such a rage that part of me feared I would never see him again—and part of me feared I most certainly *would*. In the days before our argument behind the chicken coop, I'd come as close to serenity as I had ever been; now I was walking a razor blade. One evening, seeing Evangeline alone in the park, I changed course and scuttled away, lest Finnigan be saving his reappearance for the moment I spoke to her. I saw that he was winning—that, even in absence, he was getting his wish. He was separating me from her without saying a word. I shivered in his angry shadow, chewed my nails till they bled. At night I thought of Surrender running beneath the moon, of the heat of the chase, the smell of the fear, the violent pleasure of the kill. When I slept I dreamed of Vernon, heard the soft thumping of fists.

When the front door was hammered I thought it might be him.

Dawn light buttered the walls when I opened my eyes; blearily I gathered my dressing gown and hurried down the hall. The fingers of the grandfather clock pointed to just before six. The hammering seemed loud enough to wake the dead, and I hissed through my teeth. From his bedroom came sounds of my father staggering about; no noise came from my mother's room but I knew she would have snapped awake like a bird. Despite the trouble he was causing and would cause, I knew I'd be glad when I opened the door and saw Finnigan.

But it wasn't him: it was a man with a gun.

The gun was a rifle; the man was Dockie May. Dockie was a farmer from up in the sheep hills. The Mays were rough-cut but fair people, who kept their property tidy and paid their bills on time. To see, on the doorstep, broad Dockie instead of lithe Finnigan seemed to damage my eyes. I shielded them and stepped away, away from the gun and from him. The morning sun was rich and blinding, lighting the man and the yard. "Where's your dog, son?" asked Dockie.

My shoulder knocked the wall as Father shunted me aside. He was wearing his silk dressing gown, ludicrous beside Dockie's patched shirt. He had combed his hair with his fingers, and oily tracks of their progress remained. He did not bother with greetings. He said, "Why do you want that dog, May?"

Dockie jerked his chin. "Come to my place, see. It's cut five kids to pieces."

The summer air swelled through the doorway, flipped a doily from the hall stand. Leaves tumbled and scattered across the lawn. Beyond Dockie's shoulders was a mango-orange sky, crossed with streaks of charcoal. For a moment I thought the farmer meant children, then realized he spoke of goats.

And something like a wound opened in me, and poured out dread.

My father's cheek was creased from sleep. He raised his eyebrows. "I'm a man of law, Mr. May. You need proof before you accuse even a dog of a crime. What makes you think it was our dog that killed your kids?"

"I know your dog. I seen it running loose before. I seen it in town and in this yard. I seen it this morning, just at daybreak, on the hills, running my goats to death. I fetched my gun, and I'm not sorry. Dog took off when I went after it, and I chased it back here. It's disappeared now, hiding somewhere, but the dog is yours."

My father scoffed. "You saw a dog on the hills at dawn. Lots of dogs look like our dog, especially from a distance. Our dog's four-legged and brown like the rest."

Dockie's lip jerked. He had not spent his life suffering fools. "I can prove what's right," he said. "I put a bullet in the dog that ripped my kids. Winged his shoulder, maybe his head. Your dog got a wound, it's your dog I want. The job's half-done. It needs finishing now."

"You *shot* him?"

"Go to your room," said my father to me: I shut my mouth and huddled to the wall. Father turned his gaze on the farmer. "Get on home to your goats, Dockie May. If the dog's been hurt he'll be hiding, and he'll stay hidden until you're gone."

"What about my kids? What about my losses?"

Father raised an imperious hand. "I'm not finished, May. If our dog turns up carrying a bullet wound, then we'll talk about your losses."

174

"The job needs finishing. I won't have more stock lost to him."

"If he's wounded, the job will be finished. You'll have no more trouble there."

I swayed in the hallway, a thousand hooks in my skin. I had stopped breathing long ago. Dockie was nodding grudgingly; my father stood tall and severe. As he closed the door he told the farmer, "My sympathy in regard to your goats."

I turned, then, and flew through the house. I knew where Surrender would hide. I ran barefooted across the yard, rose petals swilling in my wake. In a corner of the yard stood a woodshed where Father kept his gardening tools. I dropped to the dust by its door and peered into the space below the floor. At first I saw nothing but stars and fearsome colors swirling inside my head. Then the colors cleared and I saw his shape, the mountain range he could be. He lifted his head as high as the floor would allow, and stared at me. I reached under the shed but could not touch him. Bindi-eye dug into my knees. "Come here, Surrender," I pleaded. "Come here. . . ."

Surrender shuddered, and tucked himself tighter. Both of us heard my father's tread across the lawn— only Surrender glanced sideways to see. Each footfall brought my father closer: I wanted to whisper, *Surrender, stay there.*

But it had to be done.

Father stopped behind me. "Here, dog," he said, and slapped his knee. Surrender groaned and hesitated. Then, because he too knew it had to be done, he crept painstakingly forward. I sat back as the dog struggled out from the space and neither Father nor I said anything when we saw the red on his paws and then on his shoulder and then, when he stood, the hole in his neck. The bullet had buried under the spine, where the muscles and tendons were rope. The heat of the morning had dried the blood, clagging Surrender's coat into spikes. There was a leaf stuck in the hole, and a strand of green snapstick. I plucked these off, and Surrender twitched. I ran a hand down his head and his back, and his tail waved sorrowfully. "Good dog," I said. "Good dog."

I wiped my eyes with the heel of a hand. My father stood mute behind me. Finally he spoke: "Tie him up," he said. "When the hour's decent I'll have to borrow a gun."

There was nothing to argue: Father was a man who kept his word. I crossed the lawn and found one end of the dog chain in the grass. The links were warm from the morning sun, and speckled my palm with rust. Surrender had not moved, and did not move when I clipped the chain to his collar. My father's eyes followed me as I searched for the far end of the chain. When I found it, I dragged it to the clothesline, clipping it around the pole. I moved without blinking or thinking. My mind coasted above the trees. I tugged the chain, made sure it was secure. Surrender's head hung low; he panted. I had already decided what to do.

"You had no choice," says Finnigan.

I nod, agreeing. "I've never been lucky that way."

I trailed my father into the house and walked past him to my room. I shut the door and sat on the bed and noticed my hands were shaking. I clenched them together, crushing my fingers. There was weight on my chest, each breath a strain. I could hear the sound of china and water as my father prepared himself tea.

Unfolding my hands I saw that goat blood, or dog blood, made a pink seam in my palm.

As the kettle rattled toward boiling, I slipped from my nightclothes into shirt and trousers, and laced my boots on my feet.

Father brewed the tea, then poured it, then carried the cup to his room. I waited long minutes, my ear pressed to the door. My hearing was keen as a bat's. I heard him turning the pages of yesterday's paper. I heard him swallow the tea.

I left the room and stepped into the hall. I trod through the house in silence. In the garden I paused to unclip the chain, a hand around the dog's muzzle. He followed me at a fast-stepping lurch; together we vanished down the lane.

It was hardly dawn: Mulyan was a graveyard. The people who were awake were hunkered over stoves eating toast heaped with jam, and they gave no thought to a boy hurrying through the pink streets, a long-legged hound at his heels.

I knew where I was going. That was the extent of my plan.

We went up into the forest, Surrender and I, following first the arched backbone of Copperkettle Road, which flung like a boomerang away from town. I strode along the road that was only shallow tire-troughs, putting distance behind us as quickly as I could; Surrender trotted beside me, the bullet not slowing him down. Over our left shoulder, the town grew smaller and smaller. The scrappy bushland that lined the road soon thickened into forest, where crowded eucalypts reared creaking toward the sky. Their feet were overgrown with brittle under-brush; their shaggy reaching branches spilled bark and browning leaves. When we stepped into this forest, birds chimed in alarm. We stumbled over stone outcrops and banks of rotting logs, Surrender leaping and wriggling, my arms scratched by the unobliging scrub. We pressed through trees and hillocks of brush until I knew we were hidden from the road, that anyone walking along it wouldn't know we were near. Then I scouted for a suitable place to lie low and found a lyrebird's mound, the earth stamped and fastidiously cleared. I slumped, exhausted, gripping my ankles. I guessed that half an hour had passed since Surrender and I had left home. My skin was already tight with heat, my head beginning to thump. I wanted water, and remembered there was none.

But the trees gave us shade for the moment; for now, we were safe.

I called Surrender and we both lay down, curled on the chest of the mound. My blood moved quick through my veins. I saw Father and the empty yard, the dog chain hanging lank in his hand, my mutiny flying like a flag. I imagined how he would seethe. I put my face in Surrender's coat and closed my all-seeing eyes. In the dark I saw watercolor shades of pink, yellow, and blue. Birds had settled in the branches and their feathers snapped the air. A breeze scudded through the underbrush, scented with sap and earth. Close, I heard the dog's heartbeat, and smelled the blood in his fur. I folded my fingers around his paw and felt the warmth of his wild life. *Did you kill the kids, Surrender, as Dockie May says you did?*

Yes, and I'd do it again.

The dog fell asleep, as dogs will. I dozed, my arms a pillow. I woke up weary, and saw the canopy sway like a snake pit above me. As long as the birds continued to call, there was safety here. Ants crawled across me, and flies.

When I woke again the air was hot, and swilling like a spirit. It swelled against the forest, flexing its strength on the eucalypt trunks. My lips were dry and cracking, my teeth gritty with dust. Surrender had shifted away from me, and the lyrebird mound separated us now. He turned to watch as I sat up. The muffled colors of the forest — ocher, sienna, charcoal, khaki — made me wonder if I'd lost, in my sleep, all sharpness to my sight. I looked into the canopy and glimpsed through it a hard southern blueness of sky. The morning heat bulged and swore, trapped in the confines of the forest, a bully pinned furious to the ground.

I wiped my eyes, touched my pounding head. My arms and shoulders ached. My shirt was tacking to the flesh of my back.

Flies were blowing around Surrender's wound. He snapped at them every few moments, his teeth crashing violently. The birds had stopped calling, watching us. The breeze had ceased to weave through the canopy, and the leaves hung very still. The bush has a sound that is its own — a low, vibrant, insect buzz. It is not a welcoming, animal sound. It is the sound of indifference.

I wiped the sweat from my eyes and from the back of my knees. For a while I watched the forest. I knew we could not stay here, that thirst would catch up with us long before hunger did. I brought my knees up, hooked my arms around them. I lowered my head so I was a closed box. I hummed to myself, felt the tickling of ants.

My thoughts drifted to Evangeline.

I thought about how stupid it is, that all of us are born destined to desire somebody else, though desire brings with it such disappointment and pain. Humankind's history must be scored bloody with heartbreak. This hankering for affection is a blight upon us.

I ran my fingers across the earth. The ground, I saw, was like granite. You could not dig such sunbaked soil, not with a shovel anyway. You'd need a pick, to break its will.

I twitched; I felt I was being watched. I tried to remember when I hadn't felt that way.

I couldn't know how much time had passed since we had left home. Hours, I thought, but not many. I pictured my mother and father, their zealous, increasing outrage. I saw it first like a hurricane in the house, then realized this was wrong. There was no need for hurricanes. They'd know I must return eventually—they'd conserve their energy, and wait. I guessed that the house, like this place in the forest where Surrender and I huddled, would be quieter than it had ever been. In this silence, the grandfather clock's ticking would echo in the rooms and hall. The ticking would count off the moments until I was forced to return.

Surrender's jaws slammed shut on the flies. His tongue, between slammings, hung out. We both wanted water.

My mind went blank, like the desert. I supposed I should fight such vacancy—it seemed wrong to think of nothing. The situation, after all, was dire. It needed cunning, or distress. Nonetheless I continued to sag, boneless as a dropped puppet. The blankness was seductive, calming, handsome. It was restful as a snowfield or the rolling sea.

Great spans of time must have passed while sweat tracked pathways down my face and I made an occasional massive effort to wave away the flies.

A wattlebird flew through the forest shrieking, and roused me. I smelled the woodiness of the sun-struck trees, felt the itch of mosquito bites. I looked at Surrender, whose head was on his paws. He closed his eyes and opened them again.

If I took him home, he would die. I could not leave him here; he'd follow. If I drove him off, he'd soon come home. We would open the door and there he'd be, asleep in the shade of the veranda. He wouldn't understand that he had no home. And even if somehow I could make him understand, he would have nothing but a stray's desperate life, and soon die anyway. A farmer would shoot him, maybe catching him first in a trap. Surrender would sever his leg to escape the trap, and the farmer would follow the blood in the grass.

There was no choice to make—yet I languished, undecided.

Time crawled past on leaden hands and knees. I felt dry as if someone had skinned me. I was not the bones and meat, but the cast-aside skin. The heat had hollowed me. Sometimes I thought I was floating a whisker or two above the ground.

"Surrender," I murmured. I craned my head. It was slow and painful to turn.

His eyelids twitched, but did not open.

I peeled away spines of hair that had stuck to my throat. I crimped my toes inside my boots, felt them slip slickly against one another. Finally, I moved. I crawled, like time, on my hands and knees. The stones and twigs that littered the earth pressed into my palms. The blood stung as it was pushed through my veins.

He lifted his head as I settled beside him. There was dirt on his coat and I brushed it off. The flies circled warily, biding their time. I ran my hands over him, smoothing his ears. He felt very warm to the touch. His panting tongue was dry and pale. I lifted his lips and saw that his gums were dull pink. I leaned close to look at the wound, from which brown splashes of blood radiated. The bullet hole itself was black, crusted, dark-blue. Leaning closer still, I saw the blackness was not blood, but a blowfly. It crouched inside the warm wound hole as happily as a king. Unflustered by my waving hand, it continued to build a nursery for its creeping pallid young.

I reeled backward onto my feet, my body arched like a bow. Surrender watched me stumble on the lyre mound, strike my shoulder on a tree. I dug my fingers into the bark, a hand clamped hard to my mouth. Water came to my eyes; my empty stomach clenched and roiled. The dog watched me through pitiful eyes and I was suddenly furious that it had come to this—that he and I were alone here, abandoned to suffer. I dropped the hand and shouted. "Finnigan! Finnigan! *Finnigan!*"

I roared the word, finally, at the top of my voice. The birds scattered, the insects went mute, the wind in the trees sounded louder. I knew he was near, killing time; I knew that some dark nook concealed him and his serrated satisfaction. "Finnigan!" I screamed, and scanned fever-ishly around, circling and circling the tree. The sun was at noon above the forest, the shadows as small as could be; the branches and undergrowth seemed a painted land-scape, blanched and without depth. I shambled to a halt, dizzy. "This isn't a game!" I cried.

A gray bird—an apostle-bird—skipped from one branch to another, and spun to gaze back at me. I looked everywhere, and listened. Nothing. One by one, the force of flies returned.

"He'll die! They'll shoot him! Stop sulking, Finnigan! It's not a game!"

A scorched wind blew past me, tangling my hair. I scraped the strands from my eyes. "Finnigan?"

The word floated on the dense air, then coasted to the ground. Birds called, and shifted nervously. I stood, exhausted, dry as coal. My head ached blindingly. My arms were raw with windburn; where sweat had traveled down my cheeks the flesh felt arid as chalk. I tried to think, and my thoughts were like rabbits, paltry and flighty. I held a trembling hand to my face. I was more defeated than I had ever been. "That's your choice, then," I said to the trees. "You're the one letting him die."

I turned on my heels, clicked for Surrender. He struggled obediently to his feet, for the last time, for me.

FINNIGAN

I say, "I don't have to come when you call."

His gaze travels along the wall and stops like an ice pick on me. I hear the rattle and hitch of his breath. "Once, you said you would."

"Things had changed."

"Not that much. This wasn't a game."

"Life isn't, Gabriel."

He stares at me with his knife-blade eyes, his breath rasping and wheezing. He's realizing I'll have no mercy, that I'm here in deadly earnest—it's dawning on him that I won't back down or away. I want what I want: he has to agree. If I don't get it, I'll be angry. He sees this, and I see his jaw tighten, digging his stubbornness in. Though neither of us speaks or does anything, our hackles are up and we're snarling like two dogs ready to fight. "Don't try to be philosophical, Finnigan," he says. "It doesn't suit you."

Oh, he's feisty. I smile sweetly at him.

I don't trust him with the truth. This is what happened:

They took a few steps into the bracken and walked straight into me. I wasn't hiding. Gabriel halted, and gazed at me. His face was dark with dirt. His skin, usually white, was stained a kelpie-brown. He smiled sullenly, his mouth a fishhook: "Were you waiting for the magic word?"

Maybe I smiled too, then, soft as a tiger's paw. "Look at you," I said. "Reduced to this. Hiding in the forest. Begging for me in tears. You've messed things up, haven't you?"

"This is *your* fault," the angel answered. "You taught him to run wild."

I pushed past him and crouched beside Surrender, my Achilles' heel. I whispered and he lay down, sighing as his chest touched the earth. I ran my fingers over the wound, pressing to locate the bullet. I found it easily, a stone or nugget, lodged in muscle near the skin. Surrender moaned and struggled a little. Gabriel stood above us in rancorous silence, his hands hanging open at his sides. He was swaying, a lanky tree. "This is your fault," he said again.

I kept my hands on the dog. Without looking up at him I said, "If I do this, you'll owe me."

"Of course!" He laughed. "I wouldn't expect you to do anything from the goodness of your heart."

Like a saint, I closed my eyes. "If I take him, he'll be mine. You can't have him back."

The angel didn't answer; he swayed like a tree. He ran his knuckles down his face and tugged his knotty hair. The forest leaned against him, rose round him like a cage. Finally I felt him nod—he didn't have a choice, after all. I touched the dog, deeply pleased. Everything is mine. I skimmed a palm across the wound and in one quick movement plucked out the bullet—an art I'd learned through necessity. I heard the angel catch his breath; Surrender hardly flinched. I tossed the pellet into the scrub, saw it vanish in brown dry leaves. "All right," I murmured, and the dog clambered to his feet. I stayed crouched, patting him, tidying his fur. Gabriel stood in sulky silence; from the corner of an eye I saw a vein pulse inside his hand. Smooth and cool as water I said, "Shall I tell you what you owe me?"

"No."

Another time I would have laughed. Now I asked, "Because you already know?"

"You're wasting your time, that's why. I won't do it."

"But we agreed you owe me something if I take Surrender. You promised, Gabriel."

He stepped backward, knocking into a tree. His breathing was harsh, as it is now. I saw he was suffering, which was good. But there was still some life in him — he wasn't a husk. "Not that," he said. "No."

I sighed, very patient; then got to my feet and edged near to him. I looked into his eyes. He was watching me, biting his lip. "You've already lost me," I explained. "Just now you've lost Surrender. Do you want to lose everything, Gabriel?"

He lifted his chin. "There's nothing else worth keeping. Only her."

The wind gusted between the eucalypts, sweeping over us. "You're wrong," I said. "There are things worth keeping. Things you don't even know you have. You can still walk down the street. People don't run when they see you — not yet. You've still got your sad little life, even though you live it creeping like a rat. But things could get worse for you — don't think they could not."

"Get away from me," he said.

I gouged my eyes with frustration. "I'm trying to help you, Gabriel! That's all I've ever done."

I was close enough to see dust on his face. We looked into each other's eyes. By rights he should have dropped to his knees. Instead he said stonily, "Go away, Finnigan."

I groaned like a martyr. "What don't you understand, Gabriel? Evangeline can only hurt you. Even if she doesn't mean to, she will. Do you know why? Because she doesn't love you. She *does not love you*. It's not the way you hoped it would be."

He gazed at me with his heaven-blue eyes. "It doesn't matter," he said eventually. "Things don't have to be how I want them. Nothing's ever been that way. They've always been how *you* wanted them. My whole life has been how you wanted it to be. I didn't decide to be Gabriel. You decided for me. But that's not happening anymore, Finnigan. This is mine — *mine* — not yours. You can't have it. It belongs to me. This is how I want it."

Inside me a flicker of fury caught and burned within my bones. Calmly I said, "I'm warning you, Gabriel."

He laughed like a dog. "Warning me of *what*? How can you possibly threaten me? What's left to take? What's left to wreck? If people run when they see me, if I can't walk down the street — what difference will that make, Finnigan? *No* difference — hardly none! I'm *immune* — I'm untouchable — I'm free! You don't have to stay — you can go. I don't need your help. If I must live like something worse than a rat, I'd rather do it alone. So go on — go! Scat! Take Surrender with you. I don't need to see you again."

He shoved me with his weak arms, tears falling down his face. I stepped sideways and watched him shamble into the brush. I saw he was deranged, haywire; it did not make me pity him. I wanted to break my knuckles on his pathetic rebellion, crack his skull on his poxy immunity. I halted, watched him stagger, called, "You'll regret this, Gabriel!"

He paused, glancing backward through the leaves— then tore his way through the bracken more frantically than before. Surrender came to stand beside me, and I laid a hand on his head; we watched the angel plunge madly until the forest swallowed him whole.

GABRIEL

I've spent this long day remembering; now it's night. My recollections have reached the place beyond which I don't wish to go. Yet there'll be no point to this exhumation if I do not continue it now.

Finnigan, I see, is observing me closely. My friend now. He knows only I can save his skin. He would swear otherwise, but he's largely indifferent to the fate of my own.

I've been fearing the grave, its loneliness — yet I'm alone now. I have waited years for her to come here, but she's never arrived. I've been worried I'll lie forever unvisited, yet that's already the way things are.

Rigor mortis: deprived of their life-source oxygen, the muscle cells start to go rigid. Stiffening begins in the jaw and neck and progresses inexorably down. Within twelve hours, the frame is stiffened by a force that can be bent only by the breaking of bones. Within forty hours, it will have relaxed again.

Algor mortis: the body's temperature falls in a generally predictable way, given the environmental circumstance.

Livor mortis: red blood cells float slowly toward earth, settling in accordance with the dictates of gravity. Their congregation results in maroon staining on the areas of skin closest to the ground. Other colors will follow with time, the sedated shades of blood's limited palette. Olive, yellow, scarlet, black.

I am dreading the first heavy rain, which will seep through the soil and pool at my shoulder blades, elbows, heels. I am dreading the drip of it from the lid to my face.

I do not want to go.

My mind jumps hectically across the recollection of that last day. It lands at one memory and is horribly jolted, leaps for salvation to another, finds itself equally horrified. For this reason I've never liked recalling or speaking of that day.

After leaving the forest, I went home; I had to.

Later I left the house again; once again, I had to. "Don't tell me what happened between returning and leaving," says Finnigan. "I don't want to hear."

* * *

When I left the house again later that day, I went to Evangeline's. I was extremely disheveled after the hours spent in the forest, but I tried to tidy myself up. I stopped in the garden of a derelict house and washed my face under the tap. I remember how the water poured from the faucet as red as sundown, and how it did not soak into the dirt beneath the tap but ran away slickly, as though the ground were glass. I wet my hair and the back of my neck, scrubbed my knuckles clean on my palms. It was the middle of the afternoon, and Mulyan suffocated in silence. The heat was heavy as earth, lying weightily across my shoulders. You could not rush through such dense air — I couldn't quicken my pace beyond a walk. I met no one as I went. In the broiling heat Mulyan was crouched behind curtains, prone before fans. I walked the deserted streets and saw Christmas decorations hung around doorways, cats melting into the shade. A dog barked once as I passed, but not again. My feet in their loose boots scuffed the burning concrete. My hands felt twice their size. My mind had been hammered thin as foil and drifted somewhere near the clouds.

At her garden gate I did not linger. I remember its squeak as it turned on its hinges. The garden was deeper and wider than ours, but not so nicely decorated with flowers. I remember the path was crazy with cracks—my father would not have endured that. I remember rapping on the front door, my knuckles hurt by the timber.

I waited, breathing evenly. My eyes on the door handle. As I stood there waiting, I found I could hear music.

It was she who opened the door. She stood in the doorway, just as I'd hoped. She put a hand on her chest, where her heart would be. "Anwell," she said.

You're safe, I wanted to say; of course I couldn't—it wasn't true. It left me with nothing to say. My mind, like a kite, skinned empty air. Noise was coming from inside the house—music and laughter, competing chatter. From the doorstep I could only see Evangeline and the wall behind her, where Gainsborough was unhappily framed. But inside the house, beyond the wall, a swarm of people were gathered. I heard glass, platters, party hats. Someone blew a whistle and laughter galed down the hall. A bottle clinked, a cheek was kissed, conversation cluttered against the ceiling. "You've got visitors," I said.

She was leaning on the door, working the handle up and down. She looked lovely in her party dress. "Just a few. Just drinks—for the New Year. My parents invited them, not me."

From within the house came jeering and applause, as if the guests were being treated to a fierce puppet show. Splotches of crimson came to Evangeline's cheeks. "My parents organized it. Not me."

I nodded. It made no difference. It was not her parents I'd come to talk to, nor anyone but her. "Maybe I'll see you tomorrow, Anwell?"

I answered promptly. "No. It's important."

Her mouth bent; she glanced beyond me, into the heat-seared garden. Blasts of northern wind stripped the birch trees and flung green hearts across the lawn. The air was orange with swirling dust. She was searching for shade; there was none. Her lips twisted further— a beautiful mouth, now a scrap of barbed wire. "Come inside," she said. "But I don't have much time. I have to get back to our guests."

She held the door open and I stepped into the house. Beyond the threshold all was cushioned and cool. My smudged boots sank into carpet that was spotless, salmon-pink. On the smooth walls hung more masterpieces closed inside gilt frames. I could hear my heart thudding, taste it as though it lay on my tongue. I glanced over my shoulder, fearful of being noticed by the partygoers—I didn't want to see their faces, their curious smiles, I didn't wish to be examined like an insect on a pin. So I was relieved when the only live thing we encountered in the long walk down the hall was a child who raced by clutching his shorts and humming like a motor, vibrantly. My hands were shaking and I put them in my pockets, and the trembling skipped along my arms and pained the nerves of my teeth. Evangeline turned the handle of another door and opened it, and her bedroom was there. I hesitated, smelling nectar, realized this was no place for me. Her bedspread was of the cleanest lemon, a shade I would never have guessed. Her pillowcases were white. There was a cupboard and a dresser, and a rocking horse missing its tail. On the walls were images cut from magazines; stuffed animals ringed the room. Nothing in her bedroom was as I'd imagined it would be. I looked around and the stuffed toys gazed back, mutant, defensive, goggle-eyed. Everything was wrong here, and I felt disappointed, slightly aggrieved.

"Sit down," she said; there was a chair and she lifted up its burden of unironed clothes; then, unable to decide where to put them, dumped them back on the chair. She waved a hand loosely at the bed. "Sit there."

She seemed nervous, and I didn't want to make her more so, so I sat, gingerly. The mattress was soft as pudding. I kept my hands clamped in my lap so I would not touch anything. Like her, I was nervous, but relieved too — relieved to find her safe and well, to know I had reached her before Finnigan had. A cat-curl of breeze billowed the curtain and swilled the mobile of dolphins at the ceiling. The dolphins clattered and bobbed, knocking together plastically. Evangeline asked, "Would you like something to drink? Some water?"

"I'm fine."

"It's so hot. You look hot. Look at you: you're so . . . bedraggled."

I repeated woodenly, "I'm fine."

She stood in the center of the room, her fingers tied up in themselves. I wanted to remind her that she needn't fear me, for she seemed, unaccountably, afraid. I sensed she had arrived at a brave decision when she sat down beside me, so close our knees almost touched. A frown scarred her forehead as she said, "Has something bad happened, Anwell?"

I felt the words like an elbow to the throat. I looked away, unable to endure it — I could not have nodded or shaken my head. She had closed the door behind us and her dressing gown swayed on its hook. Beyond the door, the party sounds were muted, but nonetheless they jostled, wanting in. They crawled through the gap under the door, they poked round the window pleadingly. I looked at the carpet, which was beige. Time was getting away, and I'd been struck dumb. I looked at the toys, the dresser, the silver orb cast from the mirror onto the floor. I looked at my hands and noticed that, despite their dousing under the tap, a bead of blood had marked my thumbnail with a perfect, scarlet ring.

"My dog," I said. "Surrender."

"Surrender? Has something happened to him?"

When I came home from the forest, Surrender had not stayed behind as I'd told him . . . Finnigan had sworn to keep him, yet my father said *get the gun* . . . I had the sudden, screeching suspicion that blood had streaked me from head to toe. "Anwell!" Evangeline said sharply. "What's wrong?"

There was no blood—I saw that now. I gathered my thoughts quickly, my heart beating hard. I did not want to frighten her, but it was vital Evangeline understand and agree. At the back of my eyes I glimpsed Vernon, whom, in saving, I'd destroyed. Things would be different with Evangeline. I would make amends with Evangeline.

Then I heard Vernon say, *But I am safe, Anwell. Where I am, there's safety. Enough for her, for you.*

I jumped from the bed, strangled with panic. "Evangeline," I said, "you have to go!"

She looked dazed. "Go where?"

"Away—anywhere. You can't stay here. You have to go."

"What do you mean?" She smiled and frowned. "Anwell, I don't—"

"It's not hard to understand, Evangeline. Leave now, and don't come back."

Her gaze darted around the room. "But—why? Anwell, what—"

I shook my head, clapped my hands to my ears. There wasn't time for this—there wasn't time for her to fail to understand. I knelt on the floor in front of her. "I'm not joking, Evangeline. This isn't a game. He's coming—"

"Who? Who's coming? Anwell, stop this—"

"Just listen!" I yelped. "You need to go before he gets here. You have to hide. You have to go somewhere and not come back. Don't tell me where you're going—he'll sense that I know. He's angry. He wants revenge. So he's coming here to find you. To punish me."

The words ceased with a jolt. He was very near. In the forest he had warned I'd rue my refusal to be rid of her. Now he was near, stinking like a wolf.

Now I was doing as he'd wanted, driving her away.

I raised my eyes and saw that Evangeline's hands were around my wrists. I saw that she was frightened, yet determined to be brave. "Who is coming, Anwell? Who wants to hurt me? I'll get my father—you can tell him this—"

"No! I can't tell. He's a secret—"

She whimpered in frustration. "Who's a secret—why? You're not making sense! Who wants to punish you? What do they want with me? Tell me, Anwell—who is it? Tell me the reason—tell me the name!"

I stared at her; my heart seemed to brim. She was brave as a queen in a tower. I swore to myself that she *would* be safe; I would kill Finnigan before I let him past me. For this tiny moment we were both safe, and I lingered on my knees with my wrists in her hands. We had not often touched. Around us, the party sounds nosed and slithered. Evangeline waited for me to speak; I said nothing. "I don't understand," she eventually sighed. "You're not making any sense."

If I spoke, she would surely let go of my hands. So I stubbornly said nothing. Finnigan was coming closer, but I kept a treacherous peace. She said, "I wish you would explain."

I answered, "I can't."

"Then I don't believe you," she said.

I nodded tiredly. Her belief or disbelief would make no difference. Everything would happen regardless of her. Still, I was disappointed. If she had believed me, I would not have felt so alone. My gaze skated surfaces, avoiding her. The party sounds sniffed the door like inquisitive pets. My life was pouring out my feet and seeping through cracks in the floor; yet still I knelt and did not move, for fear she'd let go of my hands. *Let me stay,* I wanted to beg: *Please don't make me go.*

My wrists warmly wrapped in her hands; the color of her dress, which was autumn-blue; the faint sweet smell of butterscotch; the curtain wafting in the breeze. These are things I can remember.

The noise of the party abruptly changed. It had burbled and snuffled in a way that seemed friendly; suddenly it became angular and jarred. Two or three voices fluttered up, like sparrows fleeing a dogfight; the music skidded to a halt. Evangeline looked toward the door; fear splashed like lava in me. "It's him," I whispered.

"Who?" She looked from the door to me and back again. "Who?"

I scrambled up. "You've got to go. He's looking for you. And he'll hurt you, Evangeline —"

"Who?" Her voice was stringy, afraid. "Anwell!"

Now I took her wrist, and towed her to the window. She struggled, but I had no choice. The voices were swelling. They were in the hall. Nothing would slow him or turn him off course. We had almost no time. With one hand I fumbled to raise the window high. The breeze blew the curtain into the room. Evangeline struggled, grunted, and I glanced at her. "He'll kill you," I said, and she went still. Her face went white, and her struggling stilled.

It made no difference: we were out of time.

The door swung back so hard. Evangeline shrieked and scrabbled. I turned to confront Finnigan. The wind hoisted the curtain, slicked it around me. Through it I glimpsed my mother standing in the doorway, thin as a blade. "Get out, Anwell," she said.

I was stunned. I was astonished and horrified. I gazed at her, scarcely believing—for a moment I wondered if this wasn't some trick or disguise. But it was her, like antarctic gales. She had left home for the first time in months. She was not so frail as she pretended. She must have thrown back all the doors in this house until she discovered the right one. She was ruining the party. Somehow she had known I was here.

Evangeline and I stood like pillars of salt, crumbling. I must have released her wrist, for both her hands covered her mouth. The curtain sank against the wall, the dolphins bobbed against the ceiling.

My mother, not Finnigan.

The moments were solid, encased in concrete. In the hall a herd of pale faces were corralled. They leaned past each other for a better view, excited and intense. None of them moved, not a flicker—they were frozen as a stage backdrop. My mother seemed chipped out of granite. Evangeline was a doll plastered to the wall. The room was frosted over with an ice field of silence. I, too, must have been still.

Mother spoke.

"I won't tell you again, Anwell."

I stepped away from the window and Evangeline. The lemon-colored bedspread sighed as I brushed past. I crossed the threshold, through Mother's overhang, and out into the hall. A multitude of eyes scanned my face eagerly. I stared at the floor, but saw eyes and noses and mouths nonetheless. I saw the Duffs and Nightingales, the Lowes, Torquils, Gilligans, Bunkles. I saw shuffling feet and writhing hands, shoulders straining for a better view. I saw the Marcuzzi children clustered like mice.

I saw Miss Pree, the school ma'am, mistress of the fine homebrew. Daniel Collop, who had survived his youthful fast-car years to marry his beloved Lissie Skene. Constable McIllwraith, the shiny buttons of his uniform like small spot-fires. I saw these faces as I walked down the long hall and was pulled backward through my life — past neighbors, shop-keepers, councilors, sweepers, farmers, teachers, carpenters, chemists, librarians, choirboys, pot-ters, pickers, bottlers, gravediggers, junk-men, thieves — all these people who had held up my world and were now privy to it breaking apart. I saw the faces of my schoolfel-lows threaded through the crowd, their dingo eyes leveled on me, their dingo lips curved. All these whom I'd known forever now formed a guard of honorlessness for me, which stretched to the front door.

Everyone had been invited except my parents and me. *Kooksville*: Finnigan's word for it made me smile.

The front door was open, letting in the flies. I crossed into white sunlight. I had to shield my eyes. The heat pressed against me, heavy as wings.

Mother had not brought the car. She preferred not to drive. She had walked, so we walked. I followed her down the garden path and past the squeaky gate. Pigeons brows-ing on the nature-strips waddled to safety as we walked by. I kept close to Mother's side so her voice didn't need to rise. "You know I'm unwell. You know the doctor said I'm not to get upset. The entire town saw everything. You made me look a fool."

I did not really listen. I didn't see the need.

"As if things aren't bad enough for us. They all whisper about us, you know. They all talk behind our backs. Oh, they'll love this. They'll dine out on this for years."

I thought, instead, of Surrender.

"I know you're upset about your dog. But your father did what needed to be done. The dog was a killer. I won't have any more trouble. Running off, swearing, screaming. It's not good for me. The doctor says I need rest. You've heard him say so yourself. Instead I'm out here, in the blazing heat, having to bring you home. Being humiliated for my efforts. It's thoughtless, Anwell."

I thought of the unendurable shame.

Of the next day, and the next, and the next and the next and the next.

"I need my tablets. God knows, I've hardly any left. Possibly insufficient to even get me through the night. Tomorrow, you'll go to the pharmacy. You'll face these people, and your shame."

A small mutt yapped as we passed by.

At home she pushed me through the front door. I stumbled in the darkness of the hall. The pink rosebuds rained down the walls; the grandfather clock tisked crossly. My mother's form filled the doorway like spider web. "Your father's waiting for you in the kitchen." She closed the door behind her, turned over the brown key. I gazed toward the kitchen. The afternoon sun filled its doorway with stripes of bleached light. I kept a hand on the wall as I walked, dragging my fingers behind me. I was no longer steady on my feet. There was not enough left inside me to weight me firmly to the ground.

The air in the kitchen was dry. Dust capered through the stripes of light. My father was sitting at the table, a newspaper open before him. He glanced over his glasses. "She found you," he observed.

Mother had stayed in the hall.

"You know your mother is ill. It makes me wonder why you try so hard to distress her. It makes life unpleasant not only for her, but for me and yourself as well."

I flexed my fingers. They were greasy with sweat.

"We ask very little from you, Anwell. You're well provided for. You do not go without. But you will persist in being resentful, and ungrateful. You persist in behaving like a spoiled child. As such, you'll be treated accordingly. Go and get my belt."

I almost laughed. Father's belt was an old and unprincipled acquaintance from my boyhood. Like a creature of toil, it had never lived inside the house. It hung in the shed where Father kept his gardening tools. Its leather was stiff and riddled with cracks from age and neglect.

I nearly said, *I won't. I am sixteen years old.* Then I changed my mind.

I crossed the kitchen to the back door and stepped out into the yard. The sun was impossibly bright. The heat drove claws into my neck. The concrete path seemed spongy, molten. I stopped, and sank up to my ankles. The brilliant sky made me squint. The yard was quiet, the branches still. Midges hovered at the tips of the neatly mown grass. Roses slumped against each other, confetti of petals on the ground. The ducks and chickens were dozing in dust bowls beneath the trees. Their small heads came up and they watched me with wary eyes. At the side of the shed was a long lean bundle, hound-brown, motionless. Flies flew through the air around it. I wished I had something to cover him.

A knifelike sound cut the peace. Looking back to the house, I saw where it had come from. Either Mother or

Father had closed the kitchen venetian blinds. Now no one could see into the kitchen, and no one could see out.

I did not look again at the bundle on the ground. I gave it a wide berth. I went to the door of the shed and looked in. The shed was crammed with flower-pots, buckets, seedling trays, a bicycle, yet the first thing I saw was the scar-face belt hanging from its rusty hook. It was a long belt, too long for my slim father, its silver buckle more ostentatious than something he would wear. It was brown—my father preferred black. I ran my knuckles down its hide and realized that this belt had been acquired for the purpose it had always served. It wasn't meant to be worn.

I was sinking into the concrete to my shins, to my knees, yet I drifted somewhere up near the threadbare clouds. It wasn't I who, turning away, saw the hatchet resting on the tree-stump chopping block. I was elsewhere. Yet—somehow—I agreed, and approved—I must have.

Because I picked it up without a second thought.

They weren't looking when I walked into the kitchen. My mother was recounting for my father's benefit the happenings at Evangeline's. She had her back to me. "As if I don't have enough to worry about," she was saying. "You know about my health. I swear I'll go mad, I will."

It took hardly more than a flick of the wrist to bury the hatchet in her neck. Another flick to remove it. She swayed and leaned against a chair, which slid across the linoleum. "My health," she repeated, somewhat distractedly.

I scarcely paused. Even as Mother tilted, I brought the blade down on Father's skull. His mouth flopped open with the blow and I expected him to say, *Damn you*. He didn't — he kept silent. His arms twitched like landed fish and rumpled the pages of the paper.

Mother reeled away from the chair. Blood had rivered down her back. I'd always kept the hatchet sharp, as a mercy to the ducks and chickens. Now I stepped forward, and was merciful to her.

When I looked again at Father I saw that he had spilled across the table and that the newspaper was flattened with red.

It was very quiet in the kitchen now. Only I was holding my head up.

I put the hatchet on the draining board and rinsed clean my hands. My knees suddenly wobbly, I sat down on the floor. The lino was cool. Mother was tangled against the wall but the kitchen was wide, and she didn't touch me. I searched for horror or grief, repentance or surprise. But there was only a kind of exhaustion, and peevishness at the heat. My eyelids drooped; my thoughts meandered. A myna's screech dragged me back, and I pinched my hand until I was awake. I climbed to my feet and, spinning the tap, washed and dried the hatchet. I took it outside and returned it to the chopping block. The ducks and hens were still dozing in the shade. I glanced up at the kitchen window, and the closed gray venetian blinds said everything was the same.

I searched the toolshed and eventually found a piece of hessian. It was large enough, though somewhat grubby. I took it outside and spread it over the hound-brown bundle, foiling the flies. I supposed I would have to do something about digging a hole. Later, though; when it was cooler. I returned to the kitchen, to escape the heat more than anything.

The sight halted me. The streaked walls, the splattered floor, the ruby beads dropping insistently from the table to a chair. I considered the scene, chewing a nail. I opened a cupboard and rummaged through an array of cleaning fluids. From the laundry I fetched a mop and bucket.

Afterward I had to lie down on the couch. I felt tired and full of old sorrow. The harsh cleaning liquids had scalded my hands. I had opened the windows to let out the smell and from where I lay on the couch I could hear the kitchen's blinds tremble and clatter with the breeze. Toward evening the telephone rang but I didn't answer it, having nothing to say.

I may have slept; I'd been awake a long time. Since Dockie May had knocked on the door at dawn.

When night arrived and the air, though warm, was much cooler, I took a torch and went out to the shed in search of the mattock and shovel. The mattock, in particular, was vital—only it could reliably break the ground.

Even so, it was draining, digging a hole.

I took a sheet from the linen-press and used this as a shroud. I wept as I pushed the earth on top of him.

When I was finished, it was well after midnight. My work was far from done.

My father's preference for heavyset vehicles proved a blessing—the boot of the car easily held the gardening tools and other items. I worked in darkness, struggling alone, cursing, and it was hard work. Eventually, though, everything was packed. I had taken more sheets from the linen-press. Mother would have been furious.

I started the engine, hoping Mulyan slept tight. I debated whether or not to turn on the headlights—the need for secrecy seemed to suggest not. In the end I left them off until I'd passed the sign that said *Welcome to*

Mulyan, population 2014, and had turned the car toward the forest, to the dark and unfindable unknown.

Then the next day, of course, everything went wrong. There was banging and banging on the front door and I'd dragged myself down the hall before I knew where I was or what I was doing—and when I slid back the bolt there stood Constable McIllwraith, spruce as a daisy. "Anwell!" he said.

I squinted at him. Daylight made him radiant. "Good morning, Mr. McIllwraith."

"Good afternoon, you mean."

I shrugged and smiled. I meant nothing.

"I just wanted to check that you're all right."

". . . All right?"

"After yesterday."

"Yesterday?"

"That business at Evangeline's house." The Constable shuffled. "That can't have been pleasant for you."

I thought about it. "No," I agreed. "But I've known worse."

I laughed, rattly as an old cage. McIllwraith looked curiously at me. I looked at myself. My fingers, which curled around the edge of the door, were strawberry-black with yesterday's blood. The policeman asked, "Are your parents home, Anwell?"

I didn't reply. I just sighed and held the door open and let him come inside.

McIllwraith went through the house, searched the rooms, crouched to inspect cracks in the linoleum and asked question after question. I hung back, trying to be helpful. Finally he said, "You have to come with me, Anwell."

"Where to?"

"Somewhere you'll be safe. Somewhere away from here. Somewhere you can rest."

"Rest?" I said. "What for? I'm not ill."

But that was four years ago, and they told me for so long that I'm ill that now, indeed, I am. They put me in this small white room and brought Sarah here to care for me and I've been waiting ever since: waiting for Finnigan to crash through the ceiling, waiting for the bones to rise. Waiting for Evangeline to remember our friendship, but she never has.

FINNIGAN

Not a word of it makes me blink. Another time I might have savored the details; now, I'm impatient to get to the end. First, though, there's something I have to say. "That damn McIllwraith, that traitor. After everything we did for him." I think of him lying on the floor of his loungeroom, growing cold and stiff now, the flames guttered in the fireplace, the perfume gone from the air. "He should have minded his own business."

The angel's looking dreamy at the ceiling. "He used to give us cake. Remember? When we went to the station and told him where the vigilantes were going. He'd give me a slice of cake."

I ignore these ramblings. I'm thinking about the blood in the cracks of the lino floor. "*Why* did you do it?" I ask, and what I mean is not *why*, but *why then*? I know *why*. The question is why not sooner.

He speaks like wood: "There was nothing left to lose."

I nod at this, like I care. There must be an edge for everyone, over which it's possible to be pushed. My angel's pride had been trampled, his endurance worn thin. A small town is nothing but eyes and gaping maw; it pecks at its own like a flock of vicious birds. The angel must have felt cornered as a fox in a woodpile. Speaking of hiding: "You should have asked for my help. The forest's my friend. If I had given it something to hide, the forest would have kept it hidden. It wouldn't have let the rain wash away the dirt. Only moths and bats would've known the bones were there."

Gabriel smiles glassily; he's pondering his hands. He coughs unexpectedly and I think we're going to be delayed forever while he splutters and gags. I glare, and after a short while he manages to control himself. He breathes infirmly, wipes his chin on his shoulder. His blue gaze stalks the bed to me. "You'll remember the circumstances," he says, lordly as a king. "I didn't think you'd oblige, if I asked you for help."

I shrug, unruffled—I remember. I remember standing in the forest with Surrender at my heels and the angel staggering off through the trees, tilting like a gravestone. I remember thinking, *You'll regret this.* "Listen!" I bark;I resent his accusatory tone. "You're in trouble, Gabriel. The bones are found. The police are coming—they're already on their way."

I shut my mouth with a snap: I frown at him, he looks at his hands. "Yes," he says eventually, as if we're talking about the weather.

I refrain from tearing at my hair. Dignified as a river I say, "They'll want to hear your version of events. If you're not careful, they might decide this nice little room is too nice for you."

He smiles again, gives a short hitched laugh. I peer across the blanket tundra, trying to get under his skin. I hear the wheeze in-and-out from his lungs. His lungs are dark and dripping as ancient dungeon cells. I squeeze the bed frame so fiercely it bends, say, "I know why you're dying, Gabriel."

He looks at me with shards of curiosity.

"You'd rather die than live with everything that's happened. The hatchet. The humiliation."

Still he looks at me like I'm something in a jar. I wait for him to reply—he doesn't. Rancorously I suggest, "You're hoping they'll take pity on a dying boy. You're trying to look like butter wouldn't melt."

He asks, "And would it?"

I clamp my teeth. I crush the bed. I stare at the wall

until I am calm. I won't let him win. Finally, after minutes, I can look at him. I edge nearer; the bed creaks.

"You can stop dying now, Gabriel. There's no need for you to die. I'm your friend, like I always said—even when you didn't believe me. Now I've come to save you."

He watches me, asks, "How?"

I say nothing, letting him hang. Then I lean closer, slinky as a cat. "Blame McIllwraith," I say. "Tell them *he* did it. He had reason. Your father tormented him for years. The whole of Mulyan witnessed it. No one could deny that old Maccy had the motive. And—I promise you—he won't be able to say a word."

I sit back, confident; the angel looks at me. Even in the gloom I see my eyes in his own. A muffled sound treads past the door, someone restless in slippers: we hold a cautious silence as the noise slides down the hall.

The bed isn't warm, this close to him.

"But McIllwraith is our friend."

"He was treacherous at the end."

"He did what he had to do."

"Just *saying* it won't hurt him."

"He's been a truer friend to me—"

"He won't be hurt! Aren't you listening!"

"—than you have ever been."

I stare steelishly at him. "I'm trying to help you," I growl. "That's all I've ever done. That's what I'm here for—I've told you before. You've never understood."

"There's a word for your kind of help," he replies.

I smile bitterly; I won't be drawn. There's no time for sticks and stones. I look away, take my image from his eyes. We're different, me and he. I am stone and timber; he is water and feather. It charms me, how frail he is, but it also aggravates me. I won't tolerate his willful expiring. If he dies or does anything, it will be when I say he can. "Agree, Gabriel," I order. "They'll be here soon. There isn't time to muck around."

Abruptly he throws into my mind an image of a mongoose and cobra. "I like your plan," the angel says tranquilly. "It might have worked, too. McIllwraith would be another victim, but what would that matter, when there's been so many? What difference just one more? But the thing is—you guessed wrong, Finnigan. I'm not dying from shame or for sympathy or to forget what I've done. None of that matters to me. I'm dying to kill you."

He pins me with his mongoose eyes: it's exactly as I feared.

GABRIEL

I thought it would be difficult, even impossible, to will oneself to die; I've discovered that it's not. The body is a faithful servant: it knows when it's not wanted. There's nothing wrong with me—nothing found in a textbook, anyway. My illness comes from the time of chivalry and towers, of armor and sunken swords. It's a close relation to the fatally broken heart. Life is a skittish sprite—but it can be caught and tied down. It can be muzzled and deprived until its light begins to fade.

I have said, *My will be done.*

I feel no regret. Why would I? Angels are remorseless. We have one-track minds.

Finnigan is pacing the room. He is agitated. I can hear his thoughts scrabble over rocky terrain, trying to discover where he took a wrong turn. His hair is shabby as wolf's pelt; his stolen clothes don't fit. A smell rises from him— tree sap, algae. His bare heels squeak on the floor when he turns. *"Why?"* he asks plaintively. "Why would you do that? I've been such a *good* friend—what have I done wrong?"

I can tell he isn't genuinely confused—the serpentine master of the dodge and weave, he is trying to trick or trip me. A moment of uncertainty is all he needs, to plunge under my skin. But if he wants to know, I'll tell him.

"You remember that last afternoon, when I knelt on the floor in Evangeline's room? You remember the disturbance to the party—the voices, the interruption, the music turning down?"

". . . Time's ticking, Gabriel."

"I thought it was you. When I heard footsteps coming, I thought it was you. When the door opened, I thought it was you. I'd never known such terror; my heart never beat so hard. And when I saw it was my mother, *not you*—it was a relief. I was more afraid of you than of her. And I hadn't thought it was possible, Finnigan, to fear someone more than I feared her. It was, though—it was you. After that I started to wonder what good you are, if any. After that, I started to see that you shouldn't be here."

He stands motionless, gray as stone. The noise from outside is quieter now. No car sweeps by on the wet winter road and no frigid wind, ballasted with snow, wrestles in the chimney. For a moment there's peace, a gravid pause. Flatly he says, "But it wasn't me."

"It doesn't matter."

"It does. It wasn't me at the door."

I shake my head. "It doesn't matter."

He seems to spangle with rage. "You're killing me for something I didn't do!"

I will not be drawn. He understands perfectly why this must happen — after all, he is the spruiker of fear. He is the shadow in the cupboard and the whisper in the wall. Fear is Finnigan's currency, his daily wine and bread. Now he's made the mortal error of drowning himself in it. "I can't live in terror of you," I say.

"You shit," he snarls.

I'm serene. "You always underestimated me. You thought you made me harmless when you gave angelhood to me. You forgot that some angels are warriors. Where there's warriors, there's war. I will fight to the death. It's my duty. I am not afraid."

"You moron!" he screams. "You imbecile! Shut up! You'll die too — you *understand* that, don't you? If I die, *you* die!"

I smile; I'm in some pain.

Ballistic with fury he careers around the room, slamming the walls, kicking the furniture, pounding his fists on the floor. He throws the water jug across the room, exploding liquid over the walls. He wipes from the tabletop rattling bottles of pills. He snaps the drip-tube that umbilicals me, and wrestles the drip-stand to the ground. His face is mottled with anger; air whistles through his teeth. He hurls tissues, pillows, blankets, bowls . . . they hit the walls and ceiling. He reaches deadly hands for me and I say, "I wouldn't, if I were you."

"Why not?" he bawls. "What will you do, *kill me?"*

"Finnigan," I whisper, and I must barter for air; his tantrum has drained my dwindled resources . . . I've little strength left to explain. "I won't change my mind. This can't go on. It's too much damage. It has to end."

Nothing can describe his outrage; he's reduced to a black-eyed, white-fanged, wrathful silence, a dangerous thing on a chain. There's still fight in him, but he knows when he's doomed. He understands that nothing will change his destiny now. Somewhere inside him, he's mourning for himself. He dredges up a ravaged voice to say, "You deserved it. Everyone laughed at you that day. I warned you it would happen—you wouldn't listen to me.

The whole town was there to laugh. The girl Evangeline laughed. I nearly died laughing."

I nod; he's artful.

"They're still laughing at you. On the streets of Mulyan, after all these years. They say, *Remember that boy, that kooksville*. The birds are laughing. The buildings laugh. The skeletons under the gravestones laugh. Evangeline's friends are laughing."

I glance away. I'm tired. I feel his heretical gaze on me. My old, untamable friend.

"Evangeline's probably laughing," he says, "but we don't see much of her anymore. After your little exhibition that day, she asked her parents to take her away from Mulyan. The thought of you must have made her sick. She couldn't put enough distance between you and her. Maybe she caught a boat and sailed away to the other side of the world. She's as gone as gone can be. I hope you haven't been doing anything stupid, Gabriel—hoping she might come to visit you, for instance. Hoping she'll understand, forgive you, something ridiculous like that. That won't happen, never. Evangeline's gone. She's not coming back. She won't forgive you. She doesn't want to understand."

I clench my teeth, say nothing. I don't want to believe him, but I do—it makes sense, what he says. All these years of waiting for Evangeline to knock on the door, all this longing—it's wasted. I could weep, but I won't. Not now; not in front of him.

The moonlight shows the room is a shambles. Everything lies everywhere. Liquid has leaked from the torn tube of the drip and has soaked my arm and the floor. I do not speak until I'm sure my voice will be steady. "You should go, Finnigan. Surrender's waiting for you."

I feel him waver—he has one weakness. Of all the things I regret, I don't regret giving my dog to him. He's loved and tended what I could not, and kept the beloved thing safe. He crosses the room on black-pawed legs and grinds a finger into my chest. "This isn't over," he assures me. "Don't think I won't be back."

"Goodbye, Fin," I say. And I wish I was going with him, to some warm sheltered hideaway in the hills, wish that I, too, could lie down beside the dog, feel his unbroken heartbeat, smell the dust in his fur.

There's only hours. I steel my courage.

Surrender.

That roaring hot summer's day: I do not know what to call that day. The Day of the Goats, The Day in the Forest,

The Day of the Dolphins, The Day of the Hatchet. Mostly, when I think of it, I think *the last day with Surrender.*

After I had waited for Father to make the tea, after I had unchained Surrender and run through the sleeping town; after we'd climbed Copperkettle Road and found the deserted lyrebird mound; after I'd slept in the heat and woken to the silent observation of the forest, knowing that Surrender could not go home — after that, there was nothing to do but summon Finnigan, and relinquish my dog to his care. And although it was a wrench, as defeat and loss always are, I was glad that Surrender was some-where my father and Dockie May couldn't reach him.

Then I had turned and fled, blundering my way through the bracken, refusing to cede to Finnigan's demand. I would never give him victory: I would never re-nounce Evangeline. And though I ran in panic, something in me was satisfied. Finnigan, defied, could hurl threats at my back, but Surrender was safe with him: I had done a good thing.

I lurched home along Copperkettle Road, scratched, parched, exhausted. A million cicadas sang on the road-side, the wind cracked my lips. I guessed it was near midday. Finnigan's warning (*you'll regret this*) clung to my shoulders alongside the bush-flies. Occasionally I heard the cotton-ball sweep of dog paw on the road, four long brown hound-legs stepping lightly over stones and weeds. I refused to look back, covered my ears. "Stay with Finnigan," I said. "Don't follow me."

And as I drew closer to home, the tall forest petering and becoming instead the squat stained weatherboards of Mulyan's poor fringe, the sound of the paws faded until they were finally gone. His body stood beside me, true—but his spirit had returned to Finnigan. And it was spirit that mattered, I had to believe. *I had to make myself believe* the body did not matter. "Good dog," I murmured. "Stay with Finnigan."

Maybe I'd expected our house to be ruined by the strength of my father's anger at finding me absconded, the criminal Surrender unchained—I was surprised to see it standing as it always had, white and mundane. Everything looked as it always had: no passing neighbor would guess that everything had changed.

Inside, though, things were different. My mother and father sat at opposite ends of the sunroom. A mail-order gardening catalog spread across Father's lap. My mother had nothing to occupy her, so was staring into space. The room smelled of furniture polish—Father never brought his fragrant blooms inside. Mother glanced at me, fidgeted with a loose thread of the armchair. None of us said anything. The room seemed to spin on a mysterious axis; suddenly Father was in front of me. He didn't look up from his catalog. He said, "Go and ask Martin Shin for his gun."

Surrender was safe: it was possible to obey. It was easiest to obey, and have it over and done. I turned and traced my steps into the parched street.

Martin Shin lived three houses along. His house and his yard smelled rancid as cat water. Three dogs on chains barked ferociously as I approached. My mother wanted this man's house demolished. There was something inappropriate about Shin, something that belonged on the outskirts of town. Now Father was borrowing a rifle from him.

It was waiting in the hall, its slim dark muzzle touching the wall. Father had been here before me.

I was surprised by its heft when Shin set it in my hands. There was nothing to it but it was heavy, as if aware of its somber potential. Its muscle was metal, its sweat grease; its dense, proud odor rose above the reek of the house. Few things are so perfectly formed. "Be careful," Shin warned. He was dressed to go somewhere and tugged uncomfortably at his collar. "It's loaded. Don't trip on your feet when you're carrying it."

My throat was packed with gravel. My hands were bloodless as clay. "All right."

"Bring it straight back when you've finished."

"I will," I said. "Thank you."

I walked the distance of three fence lines carrying the rifle. No one saw me; no one was around. No cars passed on the road, no birds flitted through the sky. The heat draped like a lion skin on my shoulders, swirled like liquor in my wake. I thought I could hear laughter burbling from a distant TV.

At our fence I hesitated. Once, years ago, I had leaned against this fence and met a wild boy. His name, scratched into the wood, had worn away with weather and time. But he had stayed. He would never go. He would threaten to leave but he would return, volatile, unforgiving. There would never be just me alone. Where I went, so would he.

If I went to Heaven or Hell, so would he.

Father was waiting in the backyard. I walked down the garden path and his simmering stare tracked me. I stopped short of his reaching hand. He took the rifle and examined it. He prided himself on understanding the way elementary things worked. "It's loaded," I cautioned. "Beware."

In the minutes I'd been absent he'd caught and tied Surrender to the chain. Surrender dragged the links clinking through the grass and stopped beside me, his tail waving. I looked down at him, telling myself that gristle and bone were not the things that mattered. The real Surrender, I remembered, had stayed in the forest with Finnigan. Good dog.

My father pushed the rifle at me. I stepped backward, confused. Father stepped after me, proffering the weapon, his face pink with the heat. "Do it."

I stared, disbelieving. The world spun again on its unnatural axis. Gravel tumbled from my throat to my stomach, and drained out my eyes. I shook my head painstakingly. "No."

"You'll do it. It's your dog — it's your duty. You'll learn to face what must be done — not run away from it."

I stood, wavering.

The world seesawed.

"The sooner it's done, the better." It was against his law to back down.

I held up my shaking hands. My father laid the gun in them.

I could kill him with the bend of a finger. He would fall in the grass and the flies would come, sailing over the roses and out of the blue blue sky. The worms would turn, and creep as if summoned. My mother would run, afraid to look behind. It would take one moment.

Instead I looked at the dog—

—who was safe with Finnigan, I reminded myself. No matter what happened here in the yard, Surrender was safe with Finnigan. This animal before me was merely a shadow; but—

"I can't," I breathed.

"You will. It's a mercy, Anwell. It has to be done."

"Surrender," I murmured, and the dog pricked his ears. I stroked his head, smelled the wheat dust of him, all his wild traveling, all the world he'd seen. I ran a hand across the things he'd chased in his dreams, the soundness of his sleeping before the fire, the pleasure of the sun on his spine. I buried a hand in his cinnamon coat and felt his warmth in my palm. Good dog.

Good dog.

The muzzle sat neatly between his brown ears where the broad skull was near-perfectly flat.

He looked at me. I looked up; not at him.

You're Finnigan's dog now, boy.

The percussion sent the chickens haywire. I felt the body slump at my feet. Specks of blood landed on me.

I dropped the rifle and walked away. My knees and elbows creaked. Gravel was waterfalling from my pores; I left an arid river of it behind.

The house was dim inside, every curtain drawn against the heat. The kitchen radio was playing a faint tune. I wandered through the rooms, touching nothing. Everything seemed otherworldly, as if this dimension wasn't my own. Strange, the shape of a spoon and fork; strange, the flypaper hung by the window. Strange, the pattern on the loungeroom cushions, writhing, royal-blue; strange, that porcelain animals should cavort in the confines of a glass-shelved pen. I paused in the hall, snowy flowers in my head. It was hard to think past the bulging white blooms. I could hear the radio, the sound of the rifle, the hysteria of the hens.

I pressed my forehead against the wall. My arms were dotted scarlet and black. My head hurt as if crushed by iron. My fingers slid down the wall.

I reminded myself that he was safe — he was safe as could be. Finnigan had him, would never give him back, but at least he was safe. Finnigan had told me I'd regret it, but I didn't. There was peace in having nothing left to lose. That's what I knew: there was nothing left to lose.

Except Evangeline.

I realized I was on my knees, my knuckles curled on the carpet. My mother was staring down at me. Her eyes scanned me with unhappiness. "Stand up, Anwell." With effort, I did so. My thoughts ran ahead. *You'll regret this.*

"It's done, I take it?"

I nodded.

"It had to be done. It couldn't be helped. I'm sorry for it. It couldn't be helped."

I shrank from her, her diabolical pity. Flowers and darker things unfurled in my head.

"In this life, you have to take responsibility. Even for what's unpleasant. It's a lesson we each must learn, however painfully."

You'll regret this, angel. Finnigan had said that, out in the forest.

We must each learn our lesson, however painfully.

I did not regret giving Surrender to Finnigan. He must have known I wouldn't. But he'd promised I would have cause to regret *something. . . .*

I lifted my eyes. "He meant Evangeline."

Mother frowned at me. I stumbled away. He meant I would regret Evangeline. He'd meant Evangeline would regret me. I said, "Evangeline's going to pay for this."

"Anwell, stay!" my mother cried, but I was running for

the door, the street, the withered day; I made my way
through the swamp-heat of the afternoon to arrive at
Evangeline's house and told her to flee before the devil
descended from the hills and came looking, remorseless,
his ears pinned back to his sleek skull, his pitch sights set
on her.

My mother followed me and found me there, in the
bedroom, again on my knees.

Probably she was relieved to find Evangeline safe.
I suppose my words, in the hall, may have sounded
threatening. I didn't think of this at the time. It is
yet another instance of how Mother always failed to
understand me.

She ordered me home, and I followed.

Only then, home again, the day mostly gone, did I cover
the dog with hessian to give him privacy from the flies.

There's a knock on the door and my aunt Sarah comes in.
I expect her to gasp at the astonishing mess Finnigan's
made, but she apparently fails to notice it. She steps right
over the felled drip-stand, splashes without comment
through puddles on the floor. Perhaps she is simply being
kind; perhaps, in these final hours, there are things more
important than the state of the room.

She comes close to the bed, strokes my bruised arm.
She lays two fingers on my wrist, and her face, for a moment, is concentrated. It's a beautiful face, a petal. I
remember the purity of my father's flowers—the bleeding-
heart reds, the titanic whites, the Indian-spice rusts and
yellows. I feel my pulse labor, and she frowns.

I've noticed that my vision is growing cloudy, darker
than the darkening room. I've noticed a sluggishness
behind the eyes. Every atom in me feels composed of
lead. This is what dying is: a pull to the ground. I am thin
as a shadow, yet clotted as dough, my blood as thickset
as mud.

I don't want to go.

She's looking at me, brushing my hair. "If I bring some
soup, will you eat it? Will you try? Just for me, Gabriel?"

I shake my head heavily, stubborn and proud.

"Not even a spoonful?"

"No."

Sarah's mouth twists; she sighs. One of her hands
is on mine. I'm a continual source of defeat for her.
"You're safe," she says. "You know that, don't you? What
happened before—none of it matters here. Only you
matter here. Nothing that hurts you will come through
that door."

I look up at her silently. There's nothing to say. It makes her wonder if I've understood. "Not your mother or father," she adds. "Not anyone."

I glance at the door, to please her. She has such trust in it. She doesn't understand that doors, walls, fences, ceilings—they're helpless to keep out what determinedly desires to get in. My gaze slips around the room and I'm struck by how colorless everything seems. As colorless as the moon; as bleached as a talon, a warlock's cat, a child's cradle or casket. The walls, the floor, the articles, me: there's a washed-up, heavenly drabness to us all. Like an empty shell found half-buried on a beach, where I have never been.

I think I'm becoming confused. Certainly, my head aches. To the depths of their core, my bones pain.

Sarah, too, is clad in white. It's all she wears, her favorite color. "The color of peace," I breathe.

My aunt says something, shaking my arm, but I'm no longer listening. I'm imagining what it's like, to walk across sand. I look up at the ceiling, my longtime companion. Slow, slow, things are slowing down. The thunderstorm in my lungs revolves, with gigantic slowness, atop the point of a pin. There's a great congealing, a solidifying within.

I don't want to go.

I am not brave — I'm afraid. There are surely things I've always wanted to do. I am young — I must have had horizons to reach. I must have wanted to climb a sand dune. But I'm bound to this bed, there's locks on the door, I am committed, now, to my fate. My feet are washed clean, shrouded with a sheet. My fate is pooled in the center of my palms; it's blackened the bed of my nails.

I would like one last look at the world, the silver world into which Finnigan has gone. Maybe — the truth is — I wanted nothing beyond the town limits. The truth is I never dreamed of the sand. Mulyan is a tiny nondescript town, but it was large enough for me. "Sarah," I say, diving for the words, "would you open the curtain?"

She almost turns; then hesitates. Her rubber soles yelp on the floor. "Why do you always call me *Sarah*?" she asks. "You know that's not my name."

"Gabriel," I reply, "isn't mine."

"But it's what you prefer."

"My preference isn't to be who I am."

She says nothing — she studies me. Then, with a squeak of sole, she turns. The curtain is light and flies back on its cord. A haze of starlight tumbles into the room. The glass is misty with the bitter cold; beyond it broods a dingy sky. I see black steel bars spanning the height of the window. They are stalagmite and stalactite, reaching both skyward and down.

I see Vernon, outside, looking in at me.

He stands very close to the glass. His chin is level with the height of the sill. Wisps of hair float on the night air. His blue eyes are unblinking, sheened as pearls. They stare through the glass as calmly as doom.

Sarah leans on the windowsill, her face striped with shadows. She gazes thoughtfully out at the view. She hasn't noticed my brother. His eyes roll slowly up at her until the blue irises almost disappear. He stands quite still, listening to Sarah speak. He could bite her stomach, were the glass not between them. "Look at the lights," Sarah says. "Isn't the city pretty at night?"

Vernon's eyes roll liquidly down. Through the murky glass they settle on me. His hair drifts on the air. It is white and weightless. His consideration is frigid and damp. My heart jerks on its tether. "Sarah," I whisper, "come away from the window."

She does not respond. "Did you hear the commotion before? A car ran off the curb. Beeping horns: people are impatient."

Sweat has soaked the back of my neck. Vernon stares without blinking through the glass. He has not aged—he is still a child. His skull shows through the fine skin round his eyes. His flesh is luminous against the pitch night. He must be cold, but he does not shudder. His lips, which were pink, are thin yellow lines. My heart flies like a bird in a cage that's on fire. "Sarah," I hiss, "come away!"

Now Vernon is raising a hand. The tip of a finger touches the glass. He radiates no heat, the frost does not melt, he uses a nail to scratch it away.

"I don't think the driver was hurt," Sarah says.

The breeze lifts Vernon's gossamer hair. His face is empty, blanched of expression, his brow creaseless, the color of milk. His nail scrapes a crisp course through the frost, his death-mask face does not change. I should not be afraid—he always loved me—but my heart is a bird, my cool blood is cold. He has come back to me, the one who loved him, the one who stopped his insufferable life. I should be awed: I am horrified.

"A tow truck came. A big noisy thing."

ᴎ◊ᴎ月ᴲⱱ he scratches into the glass.

"Sarah!" I cry. "Come away from the window!"

"In a moment," she answers beatifically. "I'm look-ing at the lights. Hundreds and hundreds of lights. All different colors—orange, white, red, blue. Can you see them, Gabriel?"

The name in the frost is already clouded by cold. The corners of Vernon's mouth have lifted in a smile. His raised hand hovers near his chin, the fingers curled round on themselves. He seems to be waiting. He licks his lips.

Instantly I smell the smoke of Finnigan.

I struggle, mortally afraid. "Sarah," I gasp, "unbuckle the straps—"

She looks at me. "No. Gabriel, no."

I squirm like an eel, yank my arms, claw my fingers hopelessly. The bindings hold, creaking austerely, bonding my wrists to the bed's frame. I smell the scent more strongly now, the hyena seeping into the room. I kick the blankets, scrabble with my heels. Vernon watches me fight, and smiles indulgently. "Please!" I howl. "Sarah, please!"

"You know what happened last time. I nearly lost my job. Maybe, if you'd eat something, I could ask the doctors if . . ."

She talks on; I don't listen. I wrench my arms savagely, rattling the bed. I feel close to weeping with terror, close to begging like a child for the protection of my mother. A blanket bucks and slides to the floor. I taste blood on my lips and in my throat. Sarah picks up the blanket, puts her hands on her hips. "Gabriel," she says, "now stop this!"

Finally, exhausted, I go still. I lower my head. There are tears in my eyes.

Sarah smoothes the blanket over the bed. "Are you finished? Or shall I call the doctor?"

I squeeze back the tears; my wrists ache and burn. I lift my gaze and see Vernon perched silently on the end of the bed.

He is colder than the night. His body is naked, and pallid as bird skin. Every bone is traced out on him. His limbs are folded in their old, awkward way. He contemplates me with wintry interest. When he speaks, it is with Finnigan's voice. *You have two names. So do I.*

"You can go now, Sarah," I manage to say.

"I'll see you in the morning."

"Yes," I say. "Good night."

When she leaves the room, she closes the door. I hear the locks turn, unnecessarily.

Hello Anwell, says the Vernon-thing.

I dredge up my voice through the quicksand of fear: "Hello, Vernon."

The room has grown rapidly cold. The breath that clouds from me is grave-gray. The chill of him creeps up the bed. Vernon is placidly regarding the room. *This room reminds me of something. What is it, Anwell.*

His voice is metal dragged on a stone road. He never spoke, when we were boys. Now his voice is smooth, iced, untripping; familiar, like Finnigan's. And the scent of him is that of some cave-dwelling creature — a smell that was Finnigan's, leaf-mold, smoke, and clay. My heart scurries like a hunted rabbit; there's sweat beneath my eyes.

Something small white close. Something airless. Something cold. What is it, Anwell.

I don't answer: like Finnigan, he asks what he knows. I tug my arms, the bindings hold. Vernon looks blandly down the bed at me. He can't have forgiven what I did to him. How could he? There isn't forgiveness large enough to fill a small white tomb. I remember how he tumbled to the floor, blue at the lips, open-eyed, angular as books.

Anwell. I raise my eyes. His skewed hands have forged the shape of a hawk. A broken-winged hawk that would never fly, but recognizably a hawk. He chortles to himself. His hands warp round and become a stunted dog: *Yap! Yap!* he squawks. I smile encouragement, testing my bonds. My brother's fists clench and he utters a sound that tells me I'm viewing a cow. This is how he's passed the time, all these years — practicing hand puppets, in the dark, to amuse his little brother. His hands twirl; my breath catches, I see a gallows, which becomes a giraffe. He'd seen giraffes in picture books I showed him on muted Sunday afternoons when Mother's pain confined her to her bedroom and Father deadheaded his flowers. I remember it clearly, as if we sit there again: I on the floor with the book in my lap, he in his cot sucking his nightgown. I remember his face between the bars, round as an owl's, slick as a seal's. The cot was high-walled, a rattling cage.

His hands are like starfish on the linen. His pearled eyes watch me without accusation or grudge. My heart is still skittish, my blood still quick. But I loosen my fingers from the bed frame, no longer so afraid. It's comforting to see that, in his absence, my brother has hardly changed. Colder, quieter, but still him. And why should he alter? The tempests of the world haven't been his to endure. It was Finnigan who was weathered by the sun, sleet, and wind. Vernon looks as he always did, a wan celestial child. I lick my teeth and ask, "Why did you wait so long to come back?"

A sleek expression crosses his face. Not pleasure— smugness. The superiority of an older brother who revels in knowing more. *I wasn't gone. I've been here. Underneath. Underneath.*

I think of Finnigan's lithe free life, the breeze in his fingers, the sun in his eyes. His was a world of light and speed, of flame and trickery, spright and color. How much more desirable such a life would have seemed, viewed from Vernon's cramped, glacial world. How liberating it must have been, to wear a wild boy's skin.

I glance at him: he's staring at me. *Just us now, Anwell.*

He means us — Vernon and Anwell. *Like before.* Not Finnigan; not Gabriel.

I try to imagine how it could have been.

A country town is a good place for two boys to grow up in. It is safe as a cradle. The streets are broad and lined with trees; there is little traffic, and what there is travels slow. On summer evenings the air is ticked with fragments of drifting hay; in winter the smoke from chimneys douses the valley fragrantly. There is a river, which rises and falls with the rain. There are weedy, unfenced blocks of land. Here boys can catch lizards, or occasionally tiger-snakes. Boys can kick footballs to one another on the road. Neighbors keep watch over each other — a boy's sins are quickly and widely made known — and any boy's mother will tend any son's bleeding knees. There are grass hills for sliding down on a tatty piece of cardboard, there are adventure-filled dead-end lanes.

There are farms that, imploding, shed ponies and pots and pans at weekend clearing sales.

There are long, drowsy afternoons for two brothers to roam the streets unfettered, as bold and cheerfully arrogant as anybody's sons. The brothers are free to climb the steps of the store and, with coins their father gave them, buy sticks of bright chewing gum. They can race one another along the main street, ducking and weaving through the sparse crowd. A friend from school will join them in a fleetsprint to the end of the street, then return at a gallop, laughing, to his distant mother's side. The young blond brothers will wander down a side street, laboriously chewing whole packs of gum, wave to an old man drooped on a veranda, drag a stick along the footpath to make the town dogs howl. It must be a warm day, perhaps the height of summer, for the younger boy sees sunburn on the nape of his brother's slim neck. They go to the creek and wade for tadpoles and when they've trudged home in the evening, and half-heartedly eaten their tea, their mother will rub into their scuffed scorched skin a cream that smells like lavender before chasing them off to bed. They'll sleep with mouths open, and chocolate on their lips, and in their sleep they'll be entertained by colorful, perplexing dreams. Around them, the town continues ordinary and safe; this world the brothers exist within is a good, unremarkable place.

Vernon is smiling. He likes this. I know that, in a moment, he will creep slightly closer. He will creep and creep unrelentingly, until he's perched a hair's breadth from me. I'll smell his scent clearly then, the dank wood and clay. I'll see his intention sunk in his eyes. He'll want me to follow him to this world. He'll want me to dream the boys' dreams.

And why not, I wonder: why not simply go.

There are no bones in a hole inside that world, no monsters roaming the hills. The dogs doze on mats in front of the hearth; the girls are just children, harmless as butterflies.

Just a few more minutes here, I suggest: life hates to leave, worried what it might miss. But Vernon, closer, is shaking his head. *This is all.*

The air in my lungs lies coldly as soil. Facing each other, as still as we are, we're like the angels in the cemetery atop the most elaborate graves. So this is all.

I take his hand and follow him trustingly into the world. I feel sun-warmed grass growing under my feet, a cap of sunshine on my hair. At the last moment I see we're surrounded by eyes and swarthy muzzles, the ebony claws of waiting beasts. At the last moment I feel the dead weight of him, and wrench my hand from his.

He roars, enraged, grappling; darkness surges toward me. But wings unfold around me and, with a mighty sweep of air, I alone am lifted skyward, from where I first arrived.

ALSO BY SONYA HARTNETT

Stripes of the Sidestep Wolf

An American Library Association
Best Book for Young Adults

Hardcover ISBN 978-0-7636-2644-0
Paperback ISBN 978-0-7636-3416-2

What the Birds See

Hardcover
ISBN 978-0-7636-2092-9

Thursday's Child

Winner of the *Guardian*
Children's Fiction Prize

Hardcover
ISBN 978-0-7636-1620-5

Paperback
ISBN 978-0-7636-2203-9

A CLASSIC TALE BY SONYA HARTNETT

The Silver Donkey

A Book Sense Children's Pick

★ "Set in France during the Great War, *The Silver Donkey* is at once delicately told and deeply resonant. When eight-year-old Coco and ten-year-old Marcelle discover a blind and hungry soldier in the woods, they befriend him. In turn, the soldier tells tales about honesty, loyalty, courage, and kindness, all featuring a donkey. . . . This tender fable of peace will linger with both younger and older readers."

—*Publishers Weekly* (starred review)

Hardcover ISBN 978-0-7636-2937-3